MUTINY ABOARD
THE ENTERPRISE

The entire crew was deserting, hurrying down to the planet that had been declared deadly to human life.

Uhura had short-circuited all communications to Star Fleet Command. McCoy was getting blissfully drunk on mint juleps.

And Spock . . . Spock had fallen passionately in love!

Just one of the exciting stories included in this new collection, adapted from the award-winning TV series by James Blish, himself a Hugo Award winner and one of today's outstanding science fiction writers.

Bantam Books by James Blish
Ask your bookseller for the books you have missed

SPOCK MUST DIE!
STAR TREK
STAR TREK 2
STAR TREK 3
STAR TREK 4
STAR TREK 5

STAR TREK 5

ADAPTED BY JAMES BLISH

Based on the exciting television series created by Gene Roddenberry

STAR TREK 5
A Bantam Book / published February 1972
2nd printing
3rd printing
4th printing
5th printing
6th printing

Published simultaneously in the United States and Canada

Bantam Books are published by Bantam Books, Inc., a National General company. Its trade-mark, consisting of the words "Bantam Books" and the portrayal of a bantam, is registered in the United States Patent Office and in other countries. Marca Registrada. Bantam Books, Inc., 666 Fifth Avenue, New York, N.Y. 10019.

PRINTED IN THE UNITED STATES OF AMERICA

CONTENTS

PREFACE

After the announcement in *Star Trek 4* that I would be doing more of these books a year, a number of fans wrote to suggest scripts to be included—for which, again, many thanks—and in some cases to ask for a schedule of when the books would appear.

That's a question I just can't answer. I write full time for my living, and that of assorted relatives and cats, and right at this moment I have ten books in my job jar, counting this one. They all have deadlines attached, two of which I've already missed, thanks to social engagements and all the other small-shot calls of everyday life. I tend to work on two or three books concurrently, but I can't *finish* more than one at a time, and even after thirty years in this business, I find I can't predict how long any given book will take.

All that I can say for sure is that I have contracted to do four Star Trek books in the coming year, and that I'll deliver them—but exactly when each successive one will show up is something which is pretty much in the lap of the gods. I have all the scripts here, and I'll write the books, but I'll have to leave it up to you to do the watching for them.

Also, may I remind you once more that the volume of mail I get about these books is completely unprecedented in my experience, and far more than I can cope with. I read all the letters with attention and am happy to have them; but were I to try to answer them, I'd never get any books written at all. Please don't stop writing, but please also accept my apologies for not responding. As Hippocrates said about medicine: "Art is long, and time is fleeting."

JAMES BLISH

Treetops
Woodlands Road
Harpsden (Henley)
Oxon., England

WHOM GODS DESTROY

(Lee Erwin and Jerry Sohl)

Dr. Donald Cory seemed almost effusively glad to see Captain Kirk and Spock, not very much to Kirk's surprise. There was ordinary reason enough: Kirk and Governor Cory were old friends, and in addition, Kirk's official reason for the visit was to ferry him a revolutionary new drug which might release him from his bondage. And what bondage! It would take the most dedicated of men to confine himself behind a force field, beneath the poisonous atmosphere of Elba II, in order to tend the fourteen remaining incurably insane patients in the Galaxy.

"Fifteen, now," Cory said. He was a cheerful-looking man despite his duties, round-faced and white-haired. "You'll remember him, Jim: Garth of Izar."

"Of course I remember him," Kirk said, shocked. "He was one of the most brilliant cadets ever to attend the Academy. The last I heard, he was a Starship Fleet Captain—and there were no bets against his becoming an admiral, either. What happened?"

"Something utterly bizarre. He was horribly maimed in an accident off Antos IV. The people there are master surgeons, as you've probably heard. They virtually rebuilt and restored him—and in gratitude, he offered to lead them in an attempt to conquer the Galaxy. They refused, and he then tried to destroy the entire planet with all its inhabitants. One of his officers queried the order with Starfleet Command and, naturally, he wound up here."

"How is he responding?" Spock asked.

"Nobody here responds to anything we try," Cory said. "That in fact is the ultimate reason why they're here at all. Perhaps your new drug will help, but frankly, I'm pessimistic; I can't afford not to be."

"That's understandable," Kirk said. "I'd like to see Garth, Donald. Is that possible?"

"Of course. The security section is this way."

The security cells offered evidence, were any needed, that rare though insanity now was, it was no respecter of races. Most of the inmates behind the individual force fields were humanoid, but among them was a blue Andorian and a pig-faced Tellarite. Perhaps the most pathetic was a young girl, scantily dressed and quite beautiful; her greenish skin suggested that someone of Vulcan-Romulan stock had been among her ancestors, though probably a long time back, for she showed none of the other physical characteristics of those peoples.

As the group passed her, she called out urgently, "Captain! Starship Captain! You're making a mistake! Please—get me out of here and let me tell you what has happened!"

"Poor child," Cory said. "Paranoia with delusions of reference—closer to a classic pattern than anybody else we have here, but all the same we can't break through it. Captain Kirk is pressed for time at the moment, Marta."

The girl ignored him. "There's nothing wrong with me. Can't you see just by looking at me? Can't you tell just by listening to me? Why won't you let me explain?"

"A rational enough question, that last," Spock observed.

"I *am* rational!"

Kirk stopped and turned toward her. "What is it you want to say to me?"

The girl shrank away from the invisible barrier and pointed. "I can't tell you, not in front of him."

"You're afraid to talk because of Governor Cory?"

Her expression became sly, her tone confidential. "He isn't *really* Governor Cory at all, you know."

Kirk looked at Cory, who spread his hands helplessly. "I don't mean to sound callous," he said, "but I hear it every day. Everyone is plotting against her, and naturally I'm the chief villain. Garth's cell is around the corner. He's been unusually disturbed and we've had to impose additional restraints."

He waved them forward. As Kirk turned the corner, he was stunned to discover what Cory had meant by "restraints." The man in the cell was shackled spread-eagled against the wall, his chin sunk upon his chest, a vision straight out of a medieval torture chamber. With a muffled exclamation, Kirk stepped forward. Surely no modern rehabilitation program could necessitate . . .

At the sound, the prisoner looked up. He was disheveled, haggard and wild-eyed, but there could be no doubt about his identity.

He was Governor Cory.

Kirk spun. The other Cory was not there. Standing at the bend of the corridor was a tall, hawk-nosed man with deep-set, glowing eyes, with a phaser trained on the two *Enterprise* officers. Behind him crowded most of the supposedly restrained inmates Kirk had previously seen, also armed.

"Garth!"

"No other," the tall man said pleasantly. "You said you wanted to see me, Captain. Well, here I am. But I suggest you step into the cell first. The screen's down—that's why we had the Governor shackled. Tlollu, put the Vulcan in the biggest empty cell. Captain, drop your weapons on the floor and join your old friend."

Kirk had no choice. As he entered, a faint hum behind him told him that the force field had gone up. He crossed quickly to Cory and tried to release him, but the shackles turned out to be servo-driven; the control was obviously outside somewhere. Cory said hoarsely, "Sorry he tricked you, Jim."

"Don't worry, we'll think of something."

"Our esteemed Governor," Garth's voice said, "reacts to pain quite stoically, doesn't he?"

Kirk turned. The green-skinned girl was also free, and clinging to Garth, who was fondling her absently.

"Garth, you've got me. What's the point in making Cory suffer like this . . ."

"You will address me by my proper title, Kirk!"

"Sorry. I should have said Captain Garth."

"Starship Fleet Captain is merely one of my minor titles," Garth said with haughty impatience. "I am Lord Garth of Izar—and future Emperor of the Galaxy."

Oho, this was going to be very tricky; Garth had described his own madness all too accurately. "My apologies, Lord Garth."

"We forgive you. Of course, you think I'm a madman, don't you, and are humoring me. But if so, why am I out here while you two are in there?" Garth roared with laughter at his own joke. Kirk, finding the girl, Marta, watching him intently, forced a smile. She whispered in Garth's ear. "Later, perhaps. Marta seems quite taken with you, Captain Fortunately for you, I have no weaknesses, not even jealousy."

"I tried to warn you, Captain," Marta said. "Remember?"

"She did, you know," Garth said affably. "But of course I had so arranged matters that you would not listen. Our Marta is indeed a little unstable."

"What," Kirk said, "do you expect to accomplish with a staff of fourteen mad creatures?"

"Now you try reason. That is better. The Izarians, Captain, are inherently a master race. Much more so than the Romulans and the Klingons, as their failures have shown. When I return triumphantly from exile, my people will rally to my cause."

"Then you have nothing to fear from Governor Cory. Why don't you release him?"

"I fear no one; the point is well taken. You see, we can also be magnanimous." He touched a device at his belt. Behind Kirk, Cory's shackles sprang open with a clang; Kirk only just managed to catch the tortured Governor before he fell to the floor.

"Thank you, Lord Garth," Kirk said. "What have you done with the medicine I brought?"

"That poison? I destroyed it, of course. Enough of this chatter; it is time I took command of the ship you brought me. You will help me, of course."

"Why should I?"

"Because I need the ship," Garth said, with surprised patience. "My crew mutinied. So did my Fleet Captains. The first use I will make of the *Enterprise* is to hunt them down and punish them for that."

"My crew won't obey any such lunatic orders," Kirk said, abandoning with disgust any attempt to be reasonable with the poor, dangerous creature. "You're stuck, Garth. Give it up."

"Your crew will obey you, Captain. And you forget how easily I convinced *you* that I was your old friend Governor Donald Cory. It's a helpful technique, as you will observe. Watch."

Garth's features, even his very skin, seemed to crawl. When the horrifying metamorphosis was over—and it took only a few seconds—the man inside the false Cory's clothes was no longer Garth, but a mirror-Kirk.

The duplicate grinned, gave a mock salute, and strode off. Marta remained for a moment, giving Kirk a look of peculiar intensity. Then she too left, murmuring something under her breath.

"I—was praying you wouldn't get here at all," Cory said. "A starship is all he needs—and now he's got one."

"Not quite. And even if he does gain command of the *Enterprise*, one of my officers is bound to appeal his first crazy order to Starfleet Command, just as his own officers did."

"Jim, are you sure of that?"

Kirk realized that he was not at all sure of it. In the past, acting under sealed orders had forced him to give what seemed to be irrational orders often enough so that, tit for tat, his crew assumed any irrationality on his part was bound to be explained eventually. He had, in fact, long been afraid that that would be the outcome.

"No—I'm far from sure. But one starship is not a fleet; even if my officers obey him implicitly, there's a limit to the harm he can do."

"Those limits are pretty wide," Cory said. "He says he has devised a simple, compact method for making even stable suns go nova. I think it quite likely that he has. Can you imagine what a blackmail weapon that would be? And if the Izarians do rally to him—which wouldn't surprise me either, they've always been rather edgy and recalcitrant members of the Federation—then he has his fleet, too. It won't do to underestimate him, Jim."

"I don't. He was a genius, that I remember very well. What a waste!"

Cory did not answer.

"How does he manage that shape-changing trick?"

"The people of Antos taught him the technique of cellular metamorphosis and rearrangement, so he could help them restore the destroyed parts of his body. It's not uncommon in nature; on Earth, even lowly animals like crabs and starfish have it. But Garth is a long way from being a lower animal. He can mimic any form he wishes to now. He used it to kill off my entire medical staff—and to trap me. And laughed. I can still hear that laugh. And to think I hoped to rehabilitate him!"

"There's still a chance. Even masquerading as me, Garth can't get aboard the *Enterprise* without a password—we made that standard procedure after some nasty encounters with hypnosis and other forms of deception."

"Where does that leave us, Jim? He's got us."

"Why," Kirk said slowly, "he will have to ask us for help. And when that time comes, he'll get it—and it will be, with any luck at all, not the help he thinks he wants, but the help he needs."

"If you can do that," Cory said, "you're a better doctor than I am."

"I'm not a doctor at all," Kirk said. "But if I can get him into McCoy's hands . . ."

"McCoy? If you mean Leonard McCoy, he's probably Chief Medical Director of Starfleet Command by now. Hopeless."

"No, Donald. Garth is not an admiral, and McCoy is not warming any bench on Earth, either. He's in orbit right above our heads. He's the Medical Officer of the *Enterprise*."

Cory was properly staggered, but he recovered quickly. "Then," he said, "all we have to do is get Garth onto the *Enterprise*—which is exactly what he wants. I can't say that you fill me with optimism, Jim."

Garth appeared outside the cell the next day, all smiles and solicitude. "I hope you haven't been too uncomfortable, Captain?"

"I've been in worse places."

"Still, I'm afraid I've been somewhat remiss in my duties as your host. In my *persona* as Cory, I invited you down to my planet for dinner—you and Mr. Spock. The invitation still stands."

"Where is Mr. Spock?"

In answer, Garth beckoned, and Spock was brought around the corner, surrounded by an armed guard of madmen. Among them was Marta, smiling, a phaser leveled at Spock's head.

"Nice to see you, Mr. Spock."

"Thank you, Captain."

Kirk turned back to Garth. "Isn't Governor Cory dining with us?"

"Governor Cory is undergoing an involuntary fast, necessitated by his resisting me. You will find, however, that for those who cooperate we set a handsome table."

Kirk was about to refuse when Cory said, "You can't help me by going hungry, Jim. Go along with them."

"Good advice, Governor," Garth said, beaming. "Well, Captain?"

"You're very persuasive."

Garth laughed and led the way.

The staff refectory of the Elba II station had evidently been once as drably utilitarian as such places always tend to be, but now it looked like the scene of a Roman banquet. Garth waved Kirk and Spock to places between himself and Marta. They sat down wordlessly, aware of the vigilant presence at their backs of the Tellarite and the Andorian. Kirk became aware, as well, that Marta was virtually fawning on him.

Garth glared at her. "Hands off, slut."

This only seemed to please the girl. "You're jealous, after all!" she said.

"Nonsense. I'm above that sort of thing. The Captain is annoyed by your attentions. That's all."

The girl looked sweetly at Kirk. "Am I annoying you, darling?"

This looked like a good opportunity to provoke a little

dissension in the ranks of the mad. "Not really," Kirk said.

"You see? He's fascinated by me and it bothers you. Admit it."

"He said nothing of the sort," Garth retorted. "Your antics will lead to nothing but your being beaten to death."

"No, they won't. You wouldn't. I'm the most beautiful woman on this planet."

"Necessarily, since you're the only one," Garth said.

The girl preened herself. "I'm the most beautiful woman in the Galaxy. And I'm intelligent, too, and I write poetry and I paint marvelous pictures and I'm a wonderful dancer."

"Lies, all lies! Let me hear one poem you've written."

"If you like," Marta said calmly. She got up and moved to the front of the table, striking an absurdly theatrical pose. At the same time, Spock leaned slightly closer to Kirk.

"Captain," he said almost inaudibly, through motionless lips, "if you could create a diversion, I might find my way to the control room to release the force field."

Kirk nodded. The notion was a good one; all they would need would be a few seconds if Scotty had a security detail alerted—as he probably did have if Garth had already tried to pass himself off as Kirk without the password.

Garth was glaring at Marta, who, however, was looking only at Kirk. She began:

> Shall I compare thee to a summer's day?
> Thou art more lovely and more temperate.
> Rough winds do shake the darling buds of May,
> And summer's lease hath all too . . .

"*You* wrote that?" Garth broke in, shouting.

"Yesterday, as a matter of fact."

"More lies. It was written by an Earthman named Shakespeare a long time ago."

"Which doesn't change the fact that I wrote it again yesterday. I think it's one of my best poems, don't you?"

Garth controlled his temper with an obvious effort. "Sit down, Marta, you waste everyone's time. Captain, if you really want her, you can have her."

"Most magnanimous," Kirk said drily.

"You will find that I *am* magnanimous to my friends

—and merciless to my enemies. I want you, both of you, to be my friends."

"Upon what, precisely," Spock said, "will our friendship be based?"

"Upon the firmest of foundations—enlightened self-interest. You, Captain, are second only to me as the finest military commander in the Galaxy."

"That's flattering, but at present I'm primarily an explorer."

"As I have been too. I have charted more new worlds than any man in history."

"Neither of these records can help a man who has lost his judgment," Spock said coldly. "How could you, a Starship Fleet Captain, have believed that a Federation squadron would blindly obey an order to destroy the entire Antos race? That people is as famous for its benevolence as for its skill—as your own survival proves."

"That was my only miscalculation," Garth said. "I had risen above this decadent weakness, but my officers had not. My new officers, the men in this room, will obey me without question. As for you, you both have eyes but cannot see. The Galaxy surrounds us—limitless vistas—and yet the Federation would have us grub away like ants in a somewhat larger than usual anthill. But I am not an insect. I am a master, and will claim my realm."

"I agree," Kirk said, "that war is not always avoidable and that you were a great warrior. I studied your victory at Axanar when I was a cadet. It's required reading at the Academy to this day."

"Which is as it should be."

"Quite so. But my first visit to Axanar was as a newfledged lieutenant with the peace mission."

"Politicians and weaklings," Garth said. "They threw away my victory."

"No, they capped it with another. They were statesmen and humanitarians, and they had a dream—a dream that has become a reality and has spread throughout the stars. A dream that has made Mr. Spock and me brothers."

Garth smiled tightly and turned to Spock. "Do you feel that Captain Kirk is your brother?"

"Captain Kirk," Spock said, "speaks figuratively. But

with due allowance for this, what he says is logical and I do, in fact, agree with it."

"Blind—truly blind. Captain Kirk is your commanding officer and you are his subordinate; the rest is sugar-coating. But you are a worthy commander in your own right, and in my fleet you will assuredly have a starship to command."

"Forgive me," Spock said, "but exactly where *is* your fleet?"

Garth made a sweeping gesture. "Out there—waiting for me; they will flock to my cause with good reason. Limitless wealth, limitless power, solar systems ruled by the elite. We, gentlemen, are that elite. We must take what is rightfully ours from the stultifying clutches of decadence."

Spock was studying Garth with the expression of a bacteriologist confronted by a germ he had thought long extinct. "You must be aware," he said, "that you are attempting to repeat the disaster that resulted in your becoming an inmate of this place."

"I was betrayed—and then treated barbarically."

"On the contrary, you were treated justly and with a compassion you displayed toward none of your intended victims. Logically, therefore, it would . . ."

Garth bounded to his feet with a strangled cry, pointing a trembling forefinger at Spock. All other sound in the hall stopped at once.

"Remove this—this walking computer!"

Spock was removed, none too gently. Kirk's abortive move to intervene was blocked by the smiling Marta, who had produced her phaser seemingly from nowhere.

Garth took the weapon from her, and instantly switched back to his parody of the affable host. "Won't you try some of this wine, Captain?"

"Thank you, but I prefer to join Mr. Spock."

"And I prefer that you remain here. We have many divertisements more diverting than Marta's poetry, I assure you. By the way, I assume you play chess?"

"Quite a lot. We have a running tournament aboard the *Enterprise*."

"Not unusual. How would you respond to Queen to Queen's Level Three?"

So—Garth had tried to fool Scotty and had been

stopped by the code challenge; now he was fishing for the countersign. "There are, as you know, thousands of possible responses, especially if the move is not an opening one."

"I'm interested in only one."

"I can't for the life of me imagine which."

"'For the life of me' is a well-chosen phrase," Garth said, smiling silkily. "It could literally come to that, Captain."

"I doubt it. Dead I'm of no use to you at all."

"I could make you beg for death."

Kirk laughed. "Torture? You were Academy-trained, Garth. Suppose *I* attempted to break *your* conditioning by such means; would it work?"

"No," Garth admitted. "But observe, Captain, that Governor Cory is not Academy-trained, and furthermore has been weakened by his recent, ah, reverses. And among his medical equipment is a curious chair which was used in the rehabilitation process. As such it was quite painless, and, I might add, also useless. It made men docile, and hence of no use to me. I have added certain refinements to it which make it no longer painless—yet the pain can be prolonged indefinitely because there is no actual destruction of tissue."

"In the midnights of November," Marta said suddenly, "when the dead man's fair is nigh, and danger in the valley, and anger in the sky—I wrote that this morning."

"Very appropriate," Kirk said grimly.

"Tell him what he wants. Then we'll go away together."

Kirk's lips thinned. It was the old double device of the carrot and the stick, and in a very crude form, at that. But it wouldn't do to reject the carrot out of hand; the girl was obviously too unstable for that.

"Torturing Governor Cory," he said, "would be quite useless. I would simply force you to kill me; if you didn't, I would intervene."

"Phasers can be set to stun."

"If I am unconscious, I can't be blackmailed by Governor Cory's pain, can I?"

Garth glared at him for a long moment with unwinking eyes. Then a spasm of pure rage twisted his face. Raising the phaser, he leveled it at Kirk and fired point-blank.

Kirk awoke to a sound of liquid gurgling quietly. Then it stopped, and Kirk felt a cup of some sort being pressed to his lips. He swallowed automatically. Wine. Pretty good, too.

"Slowly," said a woman's voice. "Slowly, my darling."

That was Marta. He opened his eyes. He was lying on a divan with the girl sitting beside him, a goblet in her hands; there was a carafe on a small table nearby.

"Rest," she said. "You're in my room." She took his hand and kissed it gently, then stroked his face.

Kirk studied her. "So he's decided to give the carrot another try?"

"I don't understand you," she said. "I was terrified that he would put you in the Chair. I told him I would discover your secret. I lied. I would have told him anything to save you from the torment."

After a moment Kirk said, "I think you mean that."

"I do." She leaned forward and embraced him, sighing and clinging. "This is where I've longed to be. I think I knew I loved you the first moment I saw you."

Kirk disengaged himself gently. "I want to help you, Marta. If I can get back to the *Enterprise*, I'll be able to."

"It's not possible."

"There's a way," Kirk said. "If I can get to the control room and cut off the force field, Garth is finished."

"Garth is my leader."

"And he'll lead you to your destruction. He has already destroyed the medicine that might have helped you. But I think my Ship's Surgeon has a sample he might be able to duplicate."

"I will help you in a little while," Marta said thoughtfully. "Your friend Spock will soon be here, and then we will see. I've arranged that much, at any rate."

Was there no predicting this girl? "How did you do it?"

"A convincing lie," she said, shrugging, "told to a guard who finds me desirable."

"Marta, let me help you, too. If I can get away from Garth, back aboard . . ."

She silenced him with a kiss, which he did not fight. When they separated, she was breathing hard and her eyes were glittering.

"There is a way," she said. "A way in which we can

be together always. Where Garth cannot harm us. Trust me and believe in me, darling."

She kissed him again, clutching at him with almost animal intensity. At the same time, he became aware that her left hand was burrowing between the cushions of the divan. He pulled away, to discover a long, thin, wicked-looking knife which she had been about to drive into his back.

He shoved her away, hard. Almost at the same instant, Spock stepped into sight and seized her upper arms from behind.

She looked back over her shoulder. "You mustn't stop me," she said reasonably, reproachfully. "He is my love and so I must kill him. It is the only way to save him from Lord Garth."

Spock pinched her neck. The knife clattered to the floor as she slumped.

"Apparently," Spock said expressionlessly, "she has worked out an infallible method for ensuring male fidelity. An interesting aberration."

"I'm glad to see you, Mr. Spock."

"Thank you, Captain. I am now armed, and I assume we will try to reach the control room. Would you like the weapon?"

"No, I'm still a littly shaky; you handle it. The room will be guarded."

"Then we will blast our way in."

That was surprisingly ferocious of Spock; perhaps the attempted murder of his Captain had shaken him momentarily? "Only if it's absolutely necessary, Mr. Spock. Meanwhile, set your phaser on 'stun.'"

"I have already done so, Captain."

They stepped cautiously out of the room, then were forced to duck back in again as footsteps approached. Once the inmates had passed, they stole out into the corridor.

The guard before the control room was the Tellarite. He seemed to be in some sort of trance; Spock stunned him as easily as shooting a sitting duck. Kirk scooped up the fallen man's phaser, and they stuffed the limp body into a nearby closet.

Kirk cautiously tried the door. "Unlocked," he whispered. "I'll kick it open; you go in ready to shoot."

"Yes, Captain."

They burst in; but the place was deserted. Spock strode to the master switch and threw it. "Force field now off, Captain."

Kirk stationed himself at the console and activated the communicator. "Kirk to *Enterprise*. Kirk to *Enterprise*."

"Here, Captain," Uhura's voice said. "Mr. Scott, it's Captain Kirk!"

The view screen lit to show Scotty's face. "Scott here, Captain. You had us worried."

"Have Dr. McCoy synthesize a new supply of drug as fast as possible."

"Aye aye, sir."

"And I want a fully armed security detail here, Scotty, on the double."

"They're already in the Transporter Room."

"It would be better," Spock said, "if you were to return to the *Enterprise* at once."

"Why?" Kirk asked in astonishment.

"Your safety is vital to the ship. I can take charge of the security detail."

"I see," Kirk said. "Very well, Mr. Spock. Mr. Scott, beam me aboard on receipt of countersign."

"Aye, sir," the engineer said. "Queen to Queen's Level Three."

"Mr. Spock will give the countersign." Kirk leveled his phaser. "Go ahead, Spock—if that's who you are. Give him the countersign. You're supposed to know it."

"Security guard ready," Scott's voice said. "Mr. Sulu, lock into beamdown coordinates. Ensign Wyatt, ready to energize."

Spock reached for the master switch, his lineaments already changing into the less familiar ones of Garth. Kirk pulled his trigger. Nothing happened. The switch clicked home; the force field was reactivated.

"Blast away, Captain," Garth said. "I would not be fool enough to let you capture a charged phaser."

"Where is Spock? What have you done to him?"

"He is in his cell. And I have done nothing to him yet. But anything that does happen henceforth will be on your conscience—unless you give me the countersign."

"Captain Garth . . ."

"Lord Garth."

"No, sir. Captain—Starship Fleet Captain—is an honored title, and it was once yours."

"Quite true," Garth said, but his own phaser did not waver. "And I was the greatest of them all, wasn't I?"

"You were. But now you're a sick man."

Garth bristled. "I've never been more healthy."

"Think," Kirk said. "Think back. Try to remember what you were like before the accident that sent you to Antos IV."

"I—I can't remember," Garth said. "It's—almost as if I died and was reborn."

"But I remember you. You were always the finest of the Fleet Captains. You were the prototype, and a model for the rest of us."

"Yesss—I do remember that. It was a great responsibility—but one I was proud to bear."

"And you bore it well, Captain Garth, the disease that changed you is not your fault. Nor are you truly responsible for the things you've done since then—no matter how terrible they may seem to you, or to us."

"I don't want to hear any more of this," Garth said, but his voice was less decisive than his words. "You—you're weak, and you're trying to drain me of my strength."

"No! I want you to regain what you once had. I want you to go back to the greatness you lost."

For a moment Kirk thought he had been winning, but this was all too evidently the wrong tack. Garth stiffened, and the wavering phaser came back into line.

"I have never lost greatness! It was taken from me! But I shall be greater still. I am Lord Garth, Master of the Galaxy."

"Listen to me, [illegible]. . ."

"The others failed, but I will not. Alexander, Lee Kuan, Napoleon, Hitler, Krotus—all of them are dust, but I will triumph."

"Triumph or fail," Kirk said levelly, "you too will be dust."

"Not yet. Back to your cell, ex-Captain Kirk. Soon your doubts will be laid to rest. Out!"

The Tellarite and the Andorian came back for him the next day and hauled him out into the corridor, leaving

Governor Cory behind. They brought him back to the refectory, where all the rest of Garth's followers—except Marta, who was not to be seen—were working to transform the hall from a banquet scene into some sort of ceremonial chamber. Garth was there, seemingly childishly happy, dividing his attention between Kirk and his minions.

"The throne must be higher—higher than anything else. Use that table as a pedestal. Welcome back, Captain. You will be needed for our coronation."

"Coronation?" Kirk said, a little dazed.

"I know that even a real throne is merely a chair, but the symbolism is important, don't you agree? And the crown will be only a token in itself; but it will serve as a standard around which our followers will rally."

"You have only a handful of men."

Garth smiled. "Others have begun with less, but none will have reached so far as we. Good, very good. Now we will want a royal carpet for our feet. That cloth will do nicely. The tread of our feet will sanctify it."

"And it will still be a tablecloth, stained by food and wine," Kirk said. "That's all."

"My dear Captain, you do refuse to enter into the spirit of the thing, don't you? Would you prefer a larger role in the ceremony? You could serve as a human sacrifice, for example."

"I'm sure I wouldn't enjoy the rest of it. And you seem to need me alive."

"That's true. All right. How about Crown Prince?"

"I'm not part of the family. Who were they again? Krotus, Alexander, Hitler, Genghis Khan and so forth?"

"Genghis Khan," Garth said reflectively. "I'd forgotten about him. Heir apparent, I believe, that's the proper role for you. Now we think we are ready. Excuse us for the moment, Captain."

Garth bowed grandly and went out. The guards remained alert; the Tellarite, who had been stunned in Garth's earlier attempt to trick the countersign out of Kirk, was regarding the Captain with especial vigilance —and no little animosity. Evidently he had forgotten, if he had ever known, that the whole charade had been arranged by Garth himself.

Suddenly the air shook with a blast of recorded music.

Kirk did not have to be an expert to recognize it: it was, ironically, *Ich bete an die Macht der Liebe*, by somebody named Bortniansky, to which all Academy classes marched to their graduation.

The refectory doors were drawn aside, and Garth, not very resplendent in a cast off uniform, entered solemnly, chin up, eyes hooded. Beneath his right arm was tucked a crown which looked as if it had been hastily cut from a piece of sheet metal. On his right arm was Marta, swathed in trailing bedsheets and looking decidedly subdued.

The other madmen dropped to their knees, and the cold nose of a phaser against the back of his neck reminded Kirk not to remain standing alone. It came just in time—he had been almost about to laugh.

Stepping slowly in time to the processional, the "royal" couple proceeded along the "carpet" to the "throne," which they mounted. Garth turned and signaled his followers to rise. The music stopped.

"Since there is no one here, or elsewhere in the known universe, mighty enough to perform such a ceremony," he said grandly, "we will perform it ourselves. Therefore, we hereby proclaim that we are Lord Garth, formerly of Izar, now Master-that-is-to-come of the Galaxy."

He settled the metal crown upon his own head. "And now, we designate our beloved Marta to be our consort."

Garth kissed her chastely on the forehead. She shrank away from him, but stood her ground. Carefully, he fastened around her throat what appeared to be a necklace with a diamond pendant; conceivably it held the diamond from Garth's own Fleet Captain clasp, but somehow Kirk doubted that.

Garth seated himself upon the throne. "And now, guards, remove our beloved consort and our heir apparent, so that they may conclude their vital roles in this ritual."

They took Marta out first. As she was surrounded, she she began to keen—an eerie, wailing dirge that chilled Kirk's blood. They had her hands pinned behind her back.

Then the Tellarite and the Andorian were prodding

him out of the refectory, through a different door. He saw at once where he was being driven: back to the control room. Behind him, the music crashed out again, and the guards marched him along in step.

"Listen to me," he said urgently, under cover of the noise. "This may be your only chance."

They poked him with their phasers. The door to the control room loomed ahead.

"Garth will destroy all of us if you don't help me stop him," Kirk continued to the air before him. "He's using you. All he wants is power for himself. I brought you something that might have cured you, but he destroyed it."

There was no answer. Why did he continue to try reasoning with these madmen, anyhow? But at the moment there seemed to be nothing else to try.

The control room was empty. The closing of the door cut the music off. The blades of the force-field switch gleamed invitingly only a few yards away.

"If I can get a patrol in here, they'll bring more of the medicine. Garth will be finished and all of us will be safe again. Safe, and well."

Stolidly, one of the guards waved him to a chair. Kirk shrugged and sat down. There was what seemed to be an immensely long wait.

Then Garth came in, still in uniform but no longer wearing the crown. In one hand he was carrying a small flask packed with glittering crystals.

"Well done," he said to the guards. "Kirk, your resistance has now reached the point of outright stupidity, and is a considerable inconvenience to us. We propose to take sterner measures."

"If it's any further inconvenience to you, I'll be happy to cooperate."

"We shall see. Let us first introduce you to our latest invention." He tossed the flask into the air and caught it with the other hand. "This is an explosive, Captain, the most powerful one in history. Or, let us be accurate, the most powerful of all chemical explosives. This flask can vaporize the entire station; in fact, the crater it would leave would crack the crust of the planet. We trust you do not doubt our word."

"You were quite capable of such a discovery in the

past," Kirk said. "I have every reason to believe you still are."

"Good. Here!" Suddenly, Garth tossed the flask to one of the guards. Since the man had only one hand free to catch it, he very nearly dropped it. He was in great haste to throw it back to Garth, who resumed juggling it, laughing.

"How are your nerves, Captain?"

"Excellent, thank you. If it happens to me, it happens to you. That's all I need to know."

"Then we are halfway toward a solution already," Garth said. "Actually, dropping the flask would not so much as break it; the explosive must be set off electrically, from the board. But in fact, I am quite prepared to do so. Do you see why?"

"I can see that you're bluffing."

"Then your logic is deficient. Perhaps we need your friend Spock to help you reason. He is a logical man. Yes, a very logical man." Garth looked briefly at the guards. "Go and bring the Vulcan here to us."

The guards went out. Kirk felt the first surge of real hope in days. To the best of his knowledge, Spock—the real Spock—had not been taken out of his cell since his first imprisonment, when he had been confronted with impossible odds; and, being logical, had allowed himself to be taken. But in hand-to-hand combat, he was also a machine of outright inhuman efficiency. Sending only two guards to fetch him—and on top of that, aliens who probably had no experience with either the human or the Vulcan styles of infighting—was folly; or so he had to hope.

"In the meantime, Captain, let us expose the logic of the situation to you. It is your responsibility to preserve Federation lives and property—not only your life, Mr. Spock's, Governor Cory's, but that of everyone here, even including our own. You need not confirm this; as a sometime officer of the Federation—as our uniform should remind you—this was once our responsibility as well."

"It still is," Kirk said stonily.

"We have higher responsibilities now. Above all, a responsibility to our destiny. To this, you hold the key. We cannot advance further until we are in command of the *Enterprise*. Nor can we expect another such opportunity to arise in the practicable future. It might be said, in short, that if you remain stubborn, we no longer have a future, and are under no further responsibility toward it. Do you follow us so far?"

Kirk was a good distance ahead of him by now, and not at all liking what he found there. Even Spock, he suspected, would have to concede that the trap was indeed logical, however insane.

There was a buzz from the console. Moving sidewise, Garth activated a screen. Kirk could not see what it showed, but Garth obligingly told him.

"Your Vulcan friend is a most ingenious fellow. He has somehow disposed of my associates—who will suffer for their inefficiency—and is coming this way, armed. This could be most amusing."

"The joke is entirely on you," Kirk said. "You'll have no chance to play logic games now. Whichever one of us you shoot first, the other one will have you."

"Our training was as good as yours; the outcome is by no means so inevitable. Indeed, it suggests an even better scheme."

Garth moved behind Kirk, out of sight. This moved him away from the console, which he evidently reconsidered, for a moment later he went back to it—changed.

There were now two Captain Kirks. Even the uniforms were in a nearly identical state of wear and tear now. Smiling, Garth threw in all his previous cards; he even put his phaser out of reach.

Kirk tensed to spring. At the same instant, the door shot open and Spock crouched in it, phaser ready. He seemed prepared for anything except, possibly, what he found; he actually blinked in surprise.

"That's Garth," Garth said urgently, pointing. "Blast him!"

"Hold it, Spock! The madman *wants* you to shoot me!"

"Look at us carefully, Spock. Can't you tell I'm your Captain?"

"Queen to Queen Three," Spock said.

"I won't answer that. It's the one thing he wants to know."

"Very clever, Garth. I was about to say the same thing."

Spock, keeping both Kirks under the gun, crossed to the master switch.

"What are you doing?"

"Arranging to beam down a patrol," Spock said. "I should be interested to hear any objections."

"They'll walk into a trap."

"That's true, Spock. Garth can destroy the whole station instantly if he wants."

The double agreement halted the Science Officer. After a moment he said, "What maneuver did we use to defeat the Romulan torchship off Tau Centi?"

"Conchrane deceleration."

"A standard maneuver with an enemy faster than one's self. Every Starship Captain knows that."

"Agreed, Captain," Spock said to both. "Or Captains. Gentlemen, whichever one of you is Captain Garth must at this moment be expending a great deal of energy to maintain the image of Captain Kirk. That energy level cannot be maintained indefinitely. Since I am half Vulcan, I can outwait you; I have time."

"I propose a simpler solution. Shoot us both."

"Wait, Spock! I agree, he's quite right. But you must *shoot to kill*. It's the only way to ensure the safety of the *Enterprise*."

Instantly, Spock whirled on Garth and fired. Kirk sprang to the console.

"Kirk to *Enterprise* . . ."

"Scott here. Queen to Queen's Level Three."

"Queen to King's Level One."

"Aye aye, sir. Orders?"

"Beam down Dr. McCoy with the new drug supply—and the security guards with him."

"Aye, sir. Scott out."

Kirk turned. "Well done, Mr. Spock. Did you damage either of the guards seriously?"

"I fear I broke the Tellarite's arm."

"A trifle. Help me haul this hulk to the treatment room."

Garth, still unconscious, was in the same chair he had once proposed to use as an instrument of torture; Cory had stripped it of his modifications.

"Dr. McCoy, how long does this drug need to take effect?"

"Reversal of arterial and brain damage begins at once, but the rate depends on the individual. I'd say you could start as soon as—great looping comets!"

Garth had still been mimicking Kirk, even while stunned, a further evidence of his enormous personal drive. But now the change back was beginning; Kirk had forgotten that McCoy hadn't seen the process before.

"All right," McCoy said, swallowing. "Start now."

The chair whined, almost inaudibly. Then Cory cut it off. "That's all I dare give him for a starter."

Garth's eyes opened. They were peaceful but vacant, as though he had no mind left at all. They passed from one captor to another, without recognition. He began to whimper.

Kirk leaned toward him. "Captain."

Garth's moans stopped. He looked pleadingly up at Kirk.

"Captain Garth—I'm James Kirk. Perhaps you remember me."

Garth's expression, or lack of it, did not change. He looked toward Spock, and frowned slightly.

"I am a Federation Science Officer, Captain," Spock said.

"We are from the Starship *Enterprise*," Kirk said. "I am her Captain."

Garth looked back at Kirk, long and hard. Something was awakening in him, after all. He struggled to speak. Finally the mumbled words became clear.

"Federation—Starship . . ."

"Yes, sir. The *Enterprise*."

Cory was watching closely. Garth slowly reached out his hand. Kirk took it.

"A—privilege, sir. My ship is—no, cancel that. I have no ship. I am a Fleet Captain."

"My honor, Captain."

"That's enough," Cory said. He put his arms under Garth's and helped him from the chair. "Thank you, gentlemen. I can manage him now, and the rest of them, I'm sure."

As they moved off, Garth turned for a last look at

Kirk. It was now alarmingly penetrating, but still puzzled. "Should I know you, sir?" he asked.

Time for a new beginning. "No, Captain—no."

He was led out. Looking after him, Kirk said, Tell me something, Mr. Spock."

"Yes, Captain."

"Why was it so impossible to tell the difference between us?"

"It was not impossible, Captain. Our presence here is proof of that."

"Yes, and congratulations. But what took you so *long*?"

"The interval of uncertainty was actually fairly brief, Captain. It only seemed long—to you. As I threatened then, I could have waited you both out, but you made that unnecessary by proposing that I kill both of you. It was not a decision Garth could have made."

Kirk felt a faint chill. "Excuse me, Mr. Spock, but I think that's wrong. He had only just finished readying himself to destroy not only both of us, but the whole station."

"Yes, Captain, I believe he was capable of that. It would have been a grand immolation of his whole scheme. But to die by himself, ignominiously, leaving followers behind to see his defeat—no, I do not believe megalomaniacs think like that."

"I see. Well, there's no doubt about how you think."

"Indeed, sir?"

"Yes, indeed—fast. *Very* fast." Kirk raised his communicator. "Kirk to *Enterprise*. Three to beam up, Scotty."

"King," Spock added without a trace of a smile, "to King's Level One."

THE THOLIAN WEB

(Judy Burns and Chet Richards)

The bridge was at full muster—Kirk, Scott, Spock, Uhura, Chekov, Sulu—and extremely tense. The *Enterprise* was in unsurveyed territory, approaching the last reported position of the Starship *Defiant*, which had vanished without a trace three weeks ago.

"Captain," Spock said, "I have lost the use of all sensors. Were I to believe these readings, space itself is breaking up around us."

"A major failure?"

"Not in the sensors, sir; I have run a complete systems check. The failure is mine; I simply do not know how to interpret these reports."

"Captain," Scott added, "there may be no connection, but we're losing power in the warp engines."

"How bad is it?"

"We can hardly feel it now, but it's richt abnormal all the same. I canna find the cause."

Now it was Chekov's turn. "Captain, we have visual detection of an object dead ahead. It *looks* like a starship."

It did, at that, but not a starship in any condition to which they were accustomed. It was visibly shimmering.

"Mr. Spock, what's wrong with it?"

"Nonexistence, to put the matter in a word, Captain. There is virtually no radar return, mass analysis, radiation traces. We see it, but the sensors indicate it isn't there."

"Mr. Chekov, narrow the field and see if you can bring up the identification numbers. It's the *Defiant*, all right. Mr. Sulu, impulse engines only. Close to Transporter range. Lieutenant Uhura, open a hailing channel."

"I've been trying to raise them, sir, but there's no response."

Chekov shifted the viewing angle again. The other ship showed no gaping holes or other signs of damage. It was just ghostly—and silent.

"Within Transporter range, sir."

"Thanks, Mr. Sulu. Lieutenant, order Dr. McCoy to the Transporter Room. Mr. Spock, Mr. Chekov, I'll want you as well. Environment suits all around; O'Neil to handle the Transporter. Take over, Mr. Scott."

The Transporter was locked onto the bridge of the *Defiant*. The lighting there turned out to be extremely subdued; even some monitor lights were not functioning. But the situation was all too visible, nonetheless.

A man somewhat older than Kirk, wearing a captain's stripes, lay dead in his command chair, a number one phaser clutched in one hand. The other hand was twisted in the hair of a junior officer. The junior was also dead, with both his hands locked around the Captain's neck.

Chekov was the first to speak. "Has there ever been a mutiny on a starship before?"

"Technically," Spock said, "the refusal of Captain Garth's fleet to follow his orders when he became insane was a mutiny. But there has never been any record of an occurrence like this."

McCoy stopped to examine the bodies. "The Captain's neck is broken, Jim."

"This ship is still functioning," Spock said after a quick check of the communications console. "It is logical to assume that the mutineers are somewhere aboard. Yet the sensors show no sign of life anywhere in the vessel."

"Odd," Kirk said reflectively. "Very odd. Spock, you

stay here with me. Chekov, get down to Life Support and Engineering. Dr. McCoy, check out sickbay. I want some answers."

The two men moved off. As they did so, Scott's voice sounded in Kirk's helmet. "Captain, Mr. Sulu reports that he can't get an accurate fix on the *Defiant*, but it seems to be drifting away. Should he correct for range?"

Still odder. How could one ship be moving relative to the other when neither was under power? "Keep us within beaming range, but not too close."

"Chekov reporting, Captain. All dead in Life Support and in Engineering as well."

"Right. Get back up here. Bones?"

"More bodies, Jim. Proximate cause of deaths, various forms of violence. In short, I'd say they killed each other."

"Could a mental disease possibly have inflicted all of the crew at once?"

"It may still be here, sir," Chekov said, reappearing. "I feel pretty funny myself—headachy, dizzy."

"I can't answer the question," McCoy's voice said. "According to the medical log, even the ship's surgeon here didn't really know what was going on. The best I can do for you is take all the readings I can get and analyze them later. Now what the devil . . . ?"

"Bones! What's happening?"

There was a brief silence. Then: "Jim, this ship's beginning to dissolve! I just put my hand right *through* a corpse—and then through the wall next to him."

"Get back up here on the double. Kirk to *Enterprise*. Mr. Scott, stand by to beam us back."

"Captain, I can't. Not all at once, at least."

"What do you mean? What's going on over there?"

"Nothing we can understand," Scott's voice said grimly. "The *Defiant* is fading out, and it's—well, something is ripping the innards out of our own ship. It's jamming our Transporter frequencies. We've got only three working, and I can't be sure about those. One of you has got to wait."

"Request permission to remain," Spock said. "I could be completing the data."

"It's more important to get what you already have into analysis on the *Enterprise*. Don't argue. I'll probably be right after you."

But he was not. Within moments after Spock, Chekov and McCoy materialized aboard the *Enterprise*, the *Defiant* had vanished.

Scott was at the consoles with the Transporter officer. Spock joined them, removing his helmet, and scanned the board.

"See anything I don't?" Scott said.

"Apparently not. Everything is negative."

McCoy took off his own helment. "But he's got to be out there somewhere. If the Transporter won't grab him, what about the shuttlecraft? There must be some way to pick him up."

"There is no present trace of the Captain, Doctor," Spock said evenly. "The only next possible action is to feed the computer our data and see what conclusions can be drawn."

The computer was the fastest of its kind, but the wait seemed frustratingly long all the same. At last its pleasantly feminine voice said: "Integrated."

"Compute the next period of spatial interphase," Spock told it.

"Two hours, twelve minutes."

Spock shut the machine off. Scott was staring at him, aghast. "Is that how long we have to wait before we can pick up the Captain? But, Spock, I don't think I can hold the ship in place that long. The power leak is un balanced and I haven't been able to trace it, let alone stop it."

"You will have to keep trying," Spock said. "The fabric of space is very weak here. If we disturb it, there will be no chance of retrieving the Captain alive."

Chekov was looking baffled; worse, he was looking positively ill. "I don't understand," he said. "What's so special about this region of space?"

"I can only speculate," Spock said. "We exist in a universe which coexists with a multitude of others in the same physical space, but displaced in time. For certain brief periods, one area of such a space overlaps an area of ours. That is the time of interphase when we connect with the *Defiant's* universe."

"And retrieve the Captain," Uhura added.

"Perhaps. But the dimensional structure of each universe is totally dissimilar to the others. Any use of power would disturb what can at best be only a tenuous and brief connection. It might also result in our being trapped ourselves . . ."

"And die like them?" Chekov said raggedly. Suddenly his voice rose to a yell. "Damn you, Spock . . ."

He sprang. Spock, surprised, was knocked backward, Chekov's hands around his neck. Sulu attempted to drag Chekov off; the enraged man struck out at him. Scott promptly grabbed him by that arm. It was all that they could do to handle him, but the distraction enabled Spock to get in a neck pinch.

"Security guards to the bridge," Spock said to the intercom. "Dr. McCoy, will you also please report?"

McCoy appeared almost at once, taking in the scene at a glance. "He jumped you? My fault, I should have checked him the minute he said he was feeling funny, but there was so much else going on. Anybody notice any spasms of pain? Ah. What about his behavior? Hysterical? Frightened?"

"He looked more angry than frightened to me," Uhura said. "But there was nothing to be angry about."

"Nevertheless," Spock said, "there were all the signs of a murderous fury. After what we have seen aboard the *Defiant*, the episode is doubly disturbing."

"I'll say it is," McCoy said. "Guards, take him to sickbay. I'll see what I can find out from seeing the thing in its first stages. Spock, on the other subject, what makes you think Captain Kirk is still alive?"

"The Captain was locked in the Transporter beam when the *Defiant* phased out, Doctor. It is possible that he was saved the shock of transition. If we do not catch him again at the precise corresponding instant in the next interphase, he will die. There is no margin for error; his environmental unit can supply breathable air for no more than another three point twenty-six hours."

"Mr. Spock," Sulu called from the helm. "A vessel is approaching on an intercept vector."

Spock walked quickly to the command chair, and Scott went back to his post. "Status, Mr. Sulu," Spock said.

"Range, two hundred thousand kilometers and closing. Relative velocity, zero point five one C."

"Red alert," Spock said. The klaxon began to sound

throughout the ship. At the same instant, Uhura captured the intruder on the main viewing screen.

The stranger was crystalline in appearance, blue-green in coloration, and shaped like a tetrahedron within which a soft light seemed to pulsate. As the scene materialized, Sulu gasped.

"Stopped dead, Mr. Spock. Now, how do they do that? Range, ninety thousand kilometers and holding."

"Mr. Spock," Uhura said. "I'm getting a visual signal from them."

"Transfer it to the main viewer."

The scene dissolved into what might have been the command bridge of the alien vessel. Most of the frame, however, was occupied by the upper half of an unknown creature. Like its vessel, the alien was almost jewel-like in appearance, multifaceted, crystalline, though it was humanoid in build. A light pulsated rapidly but irregularly inside what seemed to be its head.

"I am Commander Loskene," the creature said at once in good Federation Intorlingua. "You are trespassing in a territorial annex of the Tholian Assembly. You must leave this area immediately."

Spock studied Loskene. The pulsating light did not seem to be in synch with the voice. He said formally, "Spock, in command of the Federation Starship *Enterprise*. Commander, the Federation regards this area as free space."

"We have claimed it. And we are prepared to use force, if necessary, to hold it."

"We are not interested in a show of force. The *Enterprise* has responded to a distress call from one of our ships and is currently engaged in rescue operations. Do you wish to assist us?"

"I find no evidence of a disabled ship. My instruments indicate that ours are the only two vessels in this area."

"The other ship is trapped in an interspatial sink. It should reappear in one hour and fifty minutes. We request that you stand by until then."

"Very well, *Enterprise*. In the interest of interstellar amity, we will wait. But we will not tolerate deceit."

The view wavered, and then the screen once more

showed the Tholian ship. Now there was nothing to do but wait—and hope.

The moment of interphase approached at last. As before, Scott personally took over the Transporter console. In the command chair, Spock watched the clock intently.

"Transporter Room."

"Aye, Mr. Spock. I'm locked onto the Captain's coordinates."

"Interphase in twenty seconds . . . ten seconds . . . five, four, three, two, one, energize!"

There was a tense silence. Then Scott's voice said, "The platform's empty, Mr. Spock. There's naught at all at those coordinates."

"Any abnormality to report, Mr. Sulu?"

"The sensor readings don't correspond to those we received the last time we saw the *Defiant*. Insofar as I can tell, the Tholian entry into the area has disturbed the interphase."

"McCoy to bridge," said the intercom. "Has the Captain been beamed aboard, Mr. Spock?"

"No, Doctor. And the interphase period has been passed. We will have to wait for the next one."

"But he hasn't got enough air for that! And there's been another case like Chekov's. I have had to confine my orderly to sickbay."

"Have you still no clues as to the cause, Doctor?"

"I know exactly what the cause is," McCoy's voice said grimly. "And there's nothing I can do to stop it. The molecular structure of the central nervous system, including the brain, is being distorted by the space we are in. Sooner or later the whole crew will be affected—unless you get the *Enterprise* out of here."

"Mr. Spock!" Sulu broke in. "We're being fired upon!"

The announcement came only seconds before the bolt itself struck. The *Enterprise* lurched, but did not roll.

"Damage control, report," Spock said.

"Minor structural damage to sections A-4 and C-13."

"Engineering, hold power steady. Mr. Sulu, divert all but emergency maintenance power into the shields."

"Sir," Sulu said, "that will reduce phaser power by fifty percent."

Almost as if it had heard him, the Tholian ship darted

forward. It seemed to be almost within touching distance before it fired again. This time, the shock threw everybody who was not seated to the floor.

"Engineering to bridge. Mr. Spock, we can't take another like that. We'll either have to fight or run."

"Mr. Sulu, lock in phaser tracking controls. Divert power to the phaser banks and fire at the next close approach. Lieutenant Uhura, open a channel to the Tholians."

McCoy came onto the bridge, his face masklike. On the main viewing screen, the pyramidal ship looped around and began another run.

"Spock, what's the use of this battle?" McCoy demanded. "You've already lost the Captain. Take the ship out of here."

Spock, intent upon the screen, did not answer. The pyramid zigzagged in. Then both vessels fired at once.

The *Enterprise* rang like a gong and the lights flickered, but the screen showed that the Tholian, too, had sustained a direct hit. There was no visible damage, but the pyramid had again stopped dead, and then began to retreat.

"A standoff," Spock said. "Mr. Scott, status?"

"Convertors burned out," Scott's voice said. "We've lost drive and hence the ability to correct drift. I estimate four hours in replacement time."

"By that time," Sulu said, "we'll have drifted right through that—that gateway out there."

"Are you satisfied?" McCoy said, picking himself up off the deck. "Spock, why did you do it?"

"To stay in the area for the next interphase," Spock said, "required for disabling the Tholian ship."

"But you're ignoring the mental effects! How can you risk your whole crew on the dim chance of rescuing one officer—one presumed dead, at that? The Captain wouldn't have done that!"

"Doctor, I hardly believe that now is the time for such comparisons. Get down to your laboratory at once and search for an antidote to the mental effects. Since we must remain here, that is your immediate task. Mine is to command the *Enterprise*."

McCoy left, though not without an angry glare.

"Mr. Spock, something has just entered sensor range,"

Sulu said. "Yes, it's another Tholian ship. Loskene must have contacted them at the same time they intercepted us. Loskene is moving back out of phaser range."

"Lieutenant, attempt contact again."

"No response, sir."

On the screen, the two Tholian ships joined—literally joined, base to base, making what seemed to be a single vessel like a six-sided diamond. Then they began to separate again. Between their previously common bases a multicolored strand stretched out across space.

Spock rose and went to the library computer station. The Tholians met again, separated, spinning another thread. Then another. Gradually, a latticework of energy seemed to be growing.

"Switch scanners, Mr. Sulu."

The screen angle changed. The tempo of the Tholian activity was speeding up rapidly. From this point of view, it seemed that the *Enterprise* was already almost a third surrounded by the web and it kept on growing.

Spock pulled his head out of the hooded viewer. "Fascinating," he said. "And very efficient. If they succeed in completing that structure before we are repaired, we shall not be able to run even if we wished to."

Nobody replied. There seemed to be nothing to say.

There was a service for Kirk. It was brief and military. Spock, as the next in command, spoke the eulogy. The speech was not long, but it was interrupted all the same, by another seizure of madness striking down a crewman in the congregation. Afterward, the tension seemed much greater.

As the rest filed out, McCoy stopped Spock at the doorway. "There is a duty to be performed in the Captain's cabin," he said. "It requires both of us."

"Then it will have to wait. My duties require my immediate return to the bridge."

"The Captain left a message tape," the surgeon said. "It was his order that it be reviewed by both of us should he ever be declared dead—as you have just done."

"It will have to wait for a more suitable moment," Spock said, putting his hand on the corridor rail.

"Why? Are you afraid it will change your present status?"

Spock turned sharply. "The mental and physical state of this crew are your responsibility, Doctor. As I have observed before, command is mine."

"Not while a last order remains to be obeyed."

For a moment Spock did not reply. Then he said, "Very well. To the Captain's quarters, then."

McCoy had evidently visited Kirk's quarters before the service, for laid out on a table was the black velvet case which contained Kirk's medals, and it was open. The surgeon looked down at them for a long moment.

"He was a hero in every sense of the word," he said. "Yet his life was sacrificed for nothing. The one thing that would have given his death meaning is the survival of the *Enterprise*. You have made that impossible."

Spock said glacially, "We came here for a specific purpose."

"Maybe not the same one. I came to find out, among other things, really why you stayed and fought."

Spock closed the box. "The Captain would have remained to recover a man at the risk of his own life, other things being equal. I do not consider the question closed."

"He wouldn't have risked the ship. And what do you mean, the question isn't closed? Do you think he may be still alive after all? Then why did you declare him dead—to assure your own captaincy?"

"Unnecessary. I am already in command of the *Enterprise*."

"It's a situation I wish I could remedy."

"If you believe," Spock said, "that I remained just to fire that phaser and kill James Kirk or this crew, it is your prerogative as Medical Officer of this ship to relieve me of duty. In the meantime, I suggest that we play the tape you referred to, so I can get back to the bridge and you can resume looking for an antidote for the madness."

"All right." McCoy turned to Kirk's viewer and flipped a switch. The screen lit; in it, Kirk was seated at his desk.

"Spock. Bones," Kirk's voice said. "Since you are playing this tape, we will assume that I am dead, the tactical situation is critical and you two are locked in mortal combat.

"It means also, Spock, that you have control of my ship and are probably making the most difficut decisions of your career. I can offer only one small piece of advice, for what it's worth. Use every scrap of knowledge and logic you've got to save the ship, but temper your judgment with intuitive insight. I believe you have that quality. But if you can't find it in yourself, then seek out McCoy. Ask his advice. And if you find it sound, take it.

"Bones, you heard what I just told Spock. Help him if you can, but remember that *he* is the Captain. His decisions, when he reaches them, are to be obeyed without further question. You might find that he is capable of both human insight and human error, and they are the most difficult to defend. But you will find that Spock is deserving of the same loyalty and confidence that you all have given me.

"As to the disposal of my personal effects . . ."

McCoy snapped the switch, and turned. For a moment the two men studied each other, less guardedly than before. Then McCoy said, "Spock, I'm sorry. It hurts, doesn't it?"

Spock closed his eyes for a moment. Then he turned and left. McCoy remained for a moment longer, thoughtful, and then stepped out into the corridor.

He was greeted by a stifled scream. Turning, he saw Uhura running toward him, half out of uniform, her normally unshakable calm dissolved in something very close to panic. She saw McCoy and stopped, gasping, trying to get words out; but before they could form, a stab of pain seemed to go through her and her knees buckled. She grabbed the rail for support.

The signs were all too clear. McCoy surreptitiously got out his hypospray, and then went to steady her.

"Lieutenant!" he said sharply. "What is it?"

"I—Doctor, I've just seen the Captain!"

"Yes, he just left a moment ago."

"No, I don't mean Mr. Spock. The captain. He's alive!"

"I'm afraid not. But of course you saw him. We would all like to see him."

Her legs were still shaking, but she seemed somewhat calmer now. "I know what you're thinking. But it isn't that. I was looking into my mirror in my quarters, and there he was. He was—sort of shimmering, like the *Defiant* was when we first saw it. He looked puzzled —and like he was trying to tell me something."

McCoy brought the hypospray up. Uhura saw it and tried to fight free, but she was too wobbly to resist. "I did see him. Tell Mr. Spock. He's alive, he's alive . . ."

The hypospray hissed. "I'll tell him," McCoy said gently. "But in the meantime, you're going to sickbay."

One of Scott's crewmen attacked him within the same hour. The effect was spreading faster through the ship. The Tholian web was now two-thirds complete, and the *Enterprise* was still without impulse drive, let alone the thrust to achieve interstellar velocity.

The crewman's attack failed; but a shaken Scott was on the bridge not ten minutes later.

"Mr. Spock—I've just seen the Captain."

"Spock to McCoy; please come to the bridge. Go on, Mr. Scott."

"He was on the upper engineering level—sparkling, rather like a Transporter effect. He seemed to be almost floating. And I think he saw us. He seemed to be breathing pretty heavily—and then, hey presto! he winked right out."

The elevator doors snapped open and McCoy came out, fast enough to pick up most of Scott's account. He said, "Scotty, are you feeling all right?"

"Och, I think so. Tired, maybe."

"So are we all, of course. Don't fail to see me if you have any other symptoms."

"Right."

"Lieutenant Uhura told a similar story before she went under," Spock said. "Perhaps we ought not to discount it entirely. Yet in critical moments, men sometimes see exactly what they want to see, even when they are not ill."

"Are you suggesting," McCoy said, "that the men are seeing the Captain because they've lost confidence in you?"

"I am making no suggestions, but merely stating a fact."

"Well, the situation is critical, all right. And there have

been more assaults on the lower decks. And if Scottie here's being affected, that will finish whatever chance we have to get the *Enterprise* out of here."

"Have you any further leads on a remedy?"

"A small one," McCoy said. "I've been toying with the idea of trying a chlortheragen derivative. But I'm not ready to try anything so drastic, yet."

"Why not?"

"Well, for one thing . . ."

"Gentlemen," Scott said quietly. "Mr. Spock. Look behind you."

At the same moment, there was a chorus of gasps from the rest of the personnel on the bridge. Spock turned.

Floating behind him was an image of Captain Kirk, full length but soapily iridescent. He seemed to recognize Spock, but to be unable to move. Kirk's hand rose to his throat, and his lips moved. There was no sound.

Spock—hurry!

The figure vanished.

The Tholian web continued to go up around the *Enterprise,* section by section. The pace had slowed somewhat; Loskene and his compatriots seemed to have concluded that the *Enterprise* would not or could not leave the area.

Aboard the ship, too, the tension seemed to have abated, if only slightly. It was now tacitly accepted that the apparition of the Captain on the bridge had not been a part of the lurking madness, and that he had been, therefore, alive then.

Spock and Scott were having another computer session.

"So your reluctance to use the phasers now stands endorsed," the Engineering Officer said. "They blasted a hole right through this crazy space fabric and sent the *Defiant* heaven only knows where."

"And would have sent the Captain with it, if we had not had a Transporter lock on him during the first fade-out. As of now, only the overlap time has changed; the next interphase will be early, in exactly twenty minutes. Can you be ready?"

"Aye," Scott said, "she'll be back together, but we'll have only eighty percent power built up."

"It will have to do."

McCoy came up behind them, carrying a tray bearing a flask and three glasses. "Compliments of the house, gentlemen," he said. "To your good health and the health of your crew. Drink it down!"

"What is it?" Spock said.

"Generally, it's an antidote-cum-preventive for the paranoid reaction. Specifically, a derivative of chlortheragen."

"If I remember aright," Scott said, "that's a nerve gas used by the Klingons. Are you trying to kill us all, McCoy?"

"I said it was a derivative, not the pure stuff. In this form it simply deadens certain nerve inputs to the brain."

"Any good brand of Scotch will do that for you."

"As a matter of fact," McCoy said, "it works best mixed with alcohol. But it does work. It even brought Chekov around, and he's been affected the longest of any of us."

Scott knocked his drink back, and made a face. "It'll nae become a regular tipple with me," he said. "I'll be getting back to my machines."

Spock nodded after him and crossed to the command chair. A moment later Chekov himself entered, beaming, and took his regular position. Uhura was already at her post, as was Sulu.

"Your absence was keenly felt, Ensign," Spock said. "To begin with, give me an estimated time for completion of the Tholian tractor field."

"At the enemy's present pace, two minutes, sir."

"Mr. Sulu, I have the computers programmed to move us through the interspatial gateway. Stand ready to resume the helm as soon as we emerge on the other side—wherever that may be."

"Transporter Room."

"Scott here."

"Ready for interphase in seventy-five seconds."

"Aye, sir, standing by."

"Mr. Spock," Sulu said, "the Tholians are getting ready to close the web. It seems to be contracting to fit the ship."

"Counting down to interphase," Chekov said. He now had an open line to the Transporter Room. "One minute."

"Mr. Scott, have we full power?"

"Only seventy-six percent, Mr. Spock."

"Can the computer call on it all at once?"

"Aye, I think she'll stand it."

"Thirty seconds."

Suddenly, on the viewing screen, between the *Enterprise*, a tiny figure in an environmental suit popped into being.

"I see him!"

"He's early!"

"It's the Captain!"

The webbing began to slide across the screen in a heavy mesh. Behind it, stars slid past as well.

"Tractor field activated," Sulu said. "We're being pulled out of here."

"Try to maintain position, Mr. Sulu."

The ship throbbed to the sudden application of power at the computer's command. Heavy tremors shook the deck.

The web vanished.

"We broke it!" Chekov cheered.

"No, Ensign, we went out through the interdimensional gateway. Since we went through shortly after interphase, we should still be in some part of normal space. Compute the distance from our original position."

"Umm—two point seventy-two parsecs." Chekov looked aghast. "But that's beyond Transporter range!"

"You forget, Mr. Chekov, that we have a shortcut. Mr. Scott, are you still locked on the Captain?"

"Aye, sir, though I dinna understand how."

"You can beam him in now—we have broken free."

"Aye, sir—got him! But he's unconscious. McCoy, this is your department."

"I will be down directly," Spock said. "Mr. Sulu, take over."

As it turned out, no elaborate treatment was needed; taking Kirk's helmet off to let him breathe ship's air removed the source of the difficulty, and once he had been moved to his quarters, an epinephrine hypospray brought him quickly to consciousness. For a moment he looked up at Spock and McCoy in silence. Then McCoy said, "Welcome home, Jim."

"Thanks, Bones. You know, I had a whole universe to myself after the *Defiant* was thrown out. There was absolutely no one else in it. Somehow I could sense it."

"That must have been disorienting," McCoy observed.

"Very. I kept trying to get through to the ship. I think I did at least three times, but it never lasted. I must say I like a crowded universe much better. How did you two get along without me?"

"We managed," McCoy said. "Spock gavc the orders. I found the answers."

Spock gave McCoy a curious glanoo, but nodded confirmation.

"You mean you didn't have any problems?" Kirk said, with slight but visible incredulity.

"Nono worth reporting, Captain," Spock said.

"Let me be tho judge of that."

"Only such minor disturbances, Captain, as are inevitable when humans are involved."

"Or are involved with Vulcans," McCoy added.

"Understood, gentlemen. I hope my last orders were helpful in solving the problems not worth reporting."

"Orders, Captain?" Spock said.

"The orders I left for you—for both of you—on tape."

"Oh, those orders!" said McCoy. "There wasn't time, Captain. We never got a chance to listen to them."

"The crisis was upon us and then passed so quickly, Captain, that . . ."

"I see," Kirk said, smiling. "Nothing worth reporting happened, and it all happened so quickly. Good. Well, let's hope there will be no similar opportunity to test those orders that you never heard. Let's get to work."

LET THAT BE YOUR LAST BATTLEFIELD

(Oliver Crawford and Lee Cronin)

An airborne epidemic was raging on Ariannus; the *Enterprise* was three hours and four minutes out from the stricken planet on a decontamination mission when her sensors picked up, of all unexpected objects, a Starfleet shuttlecraft. Furthermore, its identification numbers showed it to be the one reported stolen from Starbase 4 two weeks earlier.

Its course was very erratic, and it was leaking air. There was a humanoid creature aboard, either injured or ill. Kirk had the machine brought aboard by tractor, and then came the second surprise. The unconscious creature aboard it was, on his left side, a very black man—while his right-hand side was completely white.

Kirk and Spock, curious, watched the entity, now on the surgery's examination table, while McCoy and Nurse Chapel did what seemed indicated. This, in due course, included an injection.

"Doctor," Spock said, "is this pigmentation a natural condition of this—individual?"

"So it would seem. The black side is plain ordinary melanin."

"I never heard of such a race," Kirk said. "Spock? No? I thought not. How do you explain it, Bones?"

"At the moment, I don't."

"He looks like the outcome of a drastic argument."

"I would think not," Spock said seriously. "True, he would be difficult to account for by standard Mendelian evolution, but unaccountable rarities do occur."

"A mutation?" McCoy said. "Tenable, anyhow."

"Your prognosis, Bones?"

"Again, I can't give one. He's a novelty to me, too."

"Yet," Spock said, "you are pumping him full of your noxious potions as if he were human."

"When in doubt, the book prevails. I've run tests. Blood is blood—even when it's green like yours. The usual organs are there, somewhat rearranged, plus a few I don't recognize. But—well, judge the treatment by its fruits; he's coming around." The alien's eyes blinked open. He looked as though he were frightened, but trying not to show it.

"Touch and go there for a bit," McCoy said. "But you're no longer in danger."

"You are aboard the Starship *Enterprise*," Kirk added.

"I have heard of it," the alien said, relieved. "It is in the fleet of the United Federation of Planets?"

"Correct," Kirk said. "And so is that shuttlecraft in which you were flying."

"It was?"

"Don't you usually know whose property you're stealing?"

"I am not a thief!"

"You're certainly no ordinary thief," Kirk said, "considering what it is you appropriated."

"You are being very loose with your accusations and drawing conclusions without any facts."

"I know you made off with a ship that didn't belong to you."

"I do not 'make off' with things," the alien said, biting off the words. "My need gave me the right to its use—and note the word well, sir—the use of the ship."

Kirk shrugged. "You can try those technical evasions with Starfleet Command. You'll face your charges there."

"I am grateful that you rescued me," the alien said with sudden dignity.

"Don't mention it. We're glad we caught you. Who are you?"

"My name is Lokai."

"Go on."

"I am from the planet Cheron."

"If I remember correctly," Spock said, "that is located in the southernmost part of the Galaxy, in a quarter that is still uncharted."

"What are you doing so far from your home?" Kirk asked. Lokai did not answer. "You know that upon completion of our mission, you will be returned to Starbase to face a very serious charge."

"The charge is trifling. I would have returned the ship as soon as I had—" Lokai stopped abruptly.

"Had what? What were you planning to do?"

"You monotoned humans are all alike," Lokai said in a sudden burst of fury. "First condemn and then attack!" Struggling to get a rein on his temper, he sank back. "I will answer no more questions."

"However we view him, Captain," Spock said, "he is certainly no ordinary specimen."

Lokai looked at the First Officer as though seeing him for the first time. "A Vulcan!"

"Don't think he'll be any easier on you," McCoy said. "He's half human."

"That's a strange combination."

Spock raised one eyebrow. "Fascinating that you should think so."

"You're not like any being we've ever encountered," Kirk added. "We'd like to know more about you and your planet."

"I—I'm very tired."

"I think that's an evasion. Surely you owe your rescuers some candor."

"I insist," Lokai said, deliberately closing his eyes. "I am extremely tired. Your vindictive cross-examination has exhausted me."

Kirk looked down at the self-righteous thief for a moment. Then Chekov's voice said from the intercom, "Contact with alien ship, Captain. They request permission to beam a passenger aboard. They say it's a police matter."

"Very well. I'll see him on the bridge. Let's go, Mr. Spock."

Still another surprise awaited them there. The newcomer was almost a double for Lokai except that he was black on his right side and white on his left.

"I am Bele," he said. His manner was assured and ingratiating.

Kirk eyed him warily. "Of the planet Cheron, no doubt. What brings you to us?"

"You bear precious cargo. Lokai. He has taken refuge aboard this ship. I am here to claim him."

"All personnel on this vessel are subject to my command. No one 'claims' anyone without due process."

"My apologies," Bele said readily. "I overstepped my powers. 'Claim' was undoubtedly an unfortunate word."

"What authorization do you have and from what source?"

"I am Chief Officer of the Commission on Political Traitors. Lokai was tried for and convicted of treason, but escaped. May I see him, please?"

"He's in sickbay. Understand that since you are now aboard the *Enterprise*, you are bound by its regulations."

Bele smiled, a little cryptically. "With your permission, Captain."

There were two guards at the door of Sickbay when Kirk, Spock and Bele arrived; McCoy was inside. Lokai glared up at them.

"Well, Lokai, it's a pleasure to see you again," Bele said. "This time I'm sure our 'joining' will be of a permanent nature. Captain, you are to be congratulated. Lokai has never before been rendered so—quiescent."

Lokai made a sound remarkably like a panther snarling, which brought in the two guards in a hurry. "I'm not going back to Cheron," he said with savage anger. "It's a world of murdering oppressors."

"I told you where you were going," Kirk said. "We brought your compatriot here simply as a courtesy. He wanted to identify you."

"And you see how this killer responds," Bele said. "As he repays all his benefactors . . ."

"Benefactors?" Lokai said. "You hypocrite. Tell him how you raided our homes, tore us from our families, herded us like cattle and sold us as slaves!"

"They were savages, Captain," Bele said. "We took them into our hearts and homes and educated them."

"Yes! Just enough education to serve the Master Race."

"You were the product of our love and you repaid us with murder."

"Why should a slave have mercy on the enslaver?"

"Slave? That was changed millennia ago. You were freed."

"Freed? Were we free to be men—free to be husbands and fathers—free to live our lives in dignity and equality?"

"Yes, you were free, if you knew how to use your freedom. You were free enough to slaughter and burn all that had been built."

Lokai turned to Kirk. "I tried to break the chains of a hundred million people. My only crime is that I failed. Of that I plead guilty."

"There is an order in things," Bele said. "He asked for Utopia in a day. It can't be done."

"Not in a day. And not in ten times ten thousand years by your thinking. To you we are a loathsome breed who will never be ready. I know you and all those with whom you are plotting to take power permanently. Genocide for my people is the Utopia you plan."

Bele, his eyes wide with fury, sprang at Lokai. The guards grabbed him. "You insane, filthy little plotter of ruin! You vicious subverter of every decent thought! You're coming back to stand trial for your crimes."

"When I return to Cheron, you will understand power. I will have armies of followers."

"You were brought here to identify this man," Kirk told Bele. "It is now clear, *gentlemen*, that you know each other very well. Bringing you together is the only service this ship has to offer. It is not a battlefield."

"Captain," Lokai said, "I led revolutionaries, not criminals. I demand political asylum. Your ship is a sanctuary."

"I'll say it just once more. For you this ship is a prison."

"Captain, it is imperative that you return him for judgment."

"Cheron is not a member of the Federation. No treaties have ever been signed. Your demand to be given possession of this prisoner is impossible to honor. There are no extradition procedures to accomplish it. Is that clear, Commissioner Bele?"

"Captain," Bele said, "I hope you will be sensible."

"I'm not interested in taking sides."

"Since my vessel has left the area—I was only a paid passenger—I urge you to take us to Cheron immediately."

Kirk felt himself beginning to bristle. "This ship has a mission to perform. Millions of lives are at stake. When that is completed, I'll return to Starbase 4. You will both be turned over to the authorities. You can each make your case to them."

"I'm sorry, Captain, but that is not acceptable. Not at all!"

"As a dignitary of a far planet," Kirk said, seething, "I offer you every hospitality of the ship while you are aboard. Choose any other course, and . . ."

"You're the Captain," Bele said with sudden mildness.

"And as for you, Lokai, I suggest you rest as much as possible. Especially your vocal chords. It seems you will have a double opportunity to practice your oratory at Starbase . . ."

He was interrupted by the buzz of the intercom. "Chekov to Captain Kirk. Urgent. Will you come to the bridge, sir?"

It was urgent, all right. The ship was off course; it seemed to have taken a new heading all by itself; it was moving away from Ariannus on a tack that would wind it up in the Coal Sack if it kept up. A check with all departments failed to turn up the nature of the malfunction.

"Mr. Spock, give me the coordinates for Cheron."

"Roughly, sir, between 403 Mark 7 and Mark 9."

"Which is the way we're heading. Get Bele up here. I assigned him to the guest quarters on Deck 6."

Bele, once arrived, did not wait to be asked any questions. "Yes," he said, "we are on the way to Cheron.

I should tell you that we are not only a very old race but a very long-lived one; and we have developed special powers which you could not hope to understand. Suffice it to say that this ship is now under my direction. For a thousand of your terrestrial years I have been pursuing Lokai through the Galaxy. I haven't come this far and this long to give him up now."

The elevator doors snapped open and Lokai ran out, followed by the two security guards.

"I will not return to Cheron!" he cried despairingly. "You guaranteed me sanctuary! Captain Kirk . . ."

"He cannnot help you," Bele said. "You have lost, Lokai. You are on your way to final punishment."

"Stop him!"

"Not this time, you evil mound of filth. Not this time."

"My cause is just. You must help me—all of you . . ."

"The old cry. Pity me! Wherever he's gone, he has been helped to escape. On every planet he has found fools who bleed for him and shed tears for the oppressed one. But there is no escape from this ship. This is your last refuge."

With a cry of rage, Lokai leaped at him. Kirk pulled him off. "Security," he said, "take both of these men to the brig."

The guards stepped forward. In an instant, a visible wall of heat formed around both the aliens.

Bele laughed. "You are helpless, Captain."

"What a fool I am," Lokai said bitterly, "expecting help from such as you."

"This ship," Kirk said, "is going to Ariannus. The lives of millions of people make no other choice possible."

"You are being obtuse, Captain. I am permitting no choice. My will now controls this ship and nothing can break it." Every cord in Bele's body and every vein in his head stood out with the ferocity of his determination.

"Bele, I am Captain of this ship. It will follow whatever course I set for it—or I will order it destroyed."

Bele stared at him. "You're bluffing. You could no more destroy this ship than I could change colors."

Kirk turned sharply toward Uhura. "Lieutenant, tie bridge audio into master computer."

"Aye aye, sir."

Kirk sat down and hit a button on his chair. "Destruct Sequence. Computer, are you ready to copy?"

"Working," said the computer's voice.

"Stand by to verify Destruct Sequence Code One."

"Ready."

"This is Captain James T. Kirk of the Starship USS *Enterprise*. Destruct Sequence One—Code One One A."

There was a rapid run of lights over the face of the computer, accompanied by the usual beeping. Then on the upper left of the panel a yellow square lit up, with a black figure 1 in its center.

"Voice and Code One One A verified and correct. Sequence One complete."

"Mr. Spock, please continue."

"This is Commander Spock, Science Officer. Destruct Sequence Number Two—Code One One A Two B."

"Voice and code verified and correct. Sequence Two complete."

"Mr. Scott."

The sweat was standing out on Scott's brow. Perhaps no one aboard loved the *Enterprise* as much as he did. Looking straight into Kirk's eyes, he said mechanically, "This is Lieutenant Commander Scott, Chief Engineering Officer. Destruct Sequence Number Three—Code One B Two B Three."

"Voice and code verified and correct. Destruct Sequence engaged. Awaiting final code for thirty-second countdown."

"Mr. Spock, has this ship returned to the course set for it by my orders?"

"No, Captain. We are still headed for Cheron."

Bele said nothing. Kirk turned quietly back to the computer. "Begin thirty-second countdown. Code Zero-Zero-Destruct-Zero."

"Count beginning. Thirty. Twenty-nine."

"Now," Kirk said, "let us see you prevent the computer from fulfilling my commands."

"Twenty-five."

"You can use your will to drag this ship toward Cheron. But I control this computer. The final command is mine."

"Fifteen."

"From five to zero," Kirk said, "no command in the

universe can stop the computer from completing its Destruct order."

"Seven."

"Waiting," Kirk said relentlessly.

"Five."

The lights stopped blinking and became a steady glare, and the beeping became a continuous whine. Chekov hunched tensely over his board. Sulu's hand was white on the helm, as though he might put the ship back on course through sheer muscle power. Uhura looked at Kirk for a moment, and then her eyes closed peacefully. Spock and Scott were tensely impassive.

"Awaiting code for irrevocable five seconds," the computer's voice said.

Kirk and Bele stared at each other. Then Kirk turned back to the computer for the last time.

"Wait!" Bele said. It was a cry of despair. "I agree! I agree!"

Kirk's expression did not change. He said, "Captain James Kirk. Code One Two Three Continuity. Abort Destruct order."

"Destruct order aborted." The computer went silent.

"Mr. Spock, Are we heading for Ariannus?"

"No, sir. The *Enterprise* is now describing a circular course."

"And at Warp Seven, Captain," Scott added. "We are going nowhere mighty fast."

"I warned you of his treachery," Lokai said. "You have weapons. Kill him!"

"We are waiting, Commissioner," Kirk said, "for you to honor your commitment."

"I have an alternative solution to offer, Captain. Simple, expedient, and, I am sure, agreeable. Captain—I am happy to have you complete your mission of mercy to Ariannus. It was madness to interfere with such a worthwhile endeavor."

Kirk listened stonily.

"Please, sir. You may proceed to Ariannus. Just guarantee me that, upon completion, you will take me and my traitorous captive to Cheron."

"Sir," Kirk said, "he is not your captive—and I make no deals about control of this ship."

Bele's shoulders sagged. He closed his eyes for a

moment, his face curiously distorted, and then opened them again. "The ship's course is now in your control."

"Mr. Sulu?"

"She responds, sir. I'm resetting course for Ariannus."

"And as for you two—let me reaffirm my position. I should put both of you in the brig for what you have done. As Lokai observed, we have weapons, from which no heat shield will protect you. But I won't do it, since you are new to this part of the Galaxy, which is governed by the laws of the United Federation of Planets. We live in peace with the fullest exercise of individual rights. The need to resort to force and violence has long since passed. It will not be tolerated on this ship."

"You are both free to move about the ship. An armed guard will accompany each of you. I hope you will take the opportunity to get to know the ways of the Federation through some of its best representatives, my crew. But make no mistake. Any interference with the *function* of this ship will be severely punished. That's all."

Bele, his face inscrutable, nodded and went out, followed by a guard.

Lokai said, "You speak very well, Captain Kirk. Your words promise justice for all."

"We try, sir."

"But I have learned to wait for actions. After Ariannus—what is your justice? I shall wait to see it dispensed."

He too went out followed by a guard. Spock looked after him.

"Fascinating," the First Officer said. "Two totally hostile humanoids."

"Disgusting is what I call them," Scott said.

"That is not a scientifically accurate description," Spock said.

"Fascinating isn't one, either. And disgusting describes exactly what I feel about those two."

"Your feelings, as usual, shed no light on the matter."

"Enough for one day," Kirk said. "Those two are beginning to affect you."

Lokai settled upon Uhura as his next hope, perhaps feeling that since he had made no headway with the white members of the crew, a black one might be more sympathetic. He was talking eagerly to her in the rec room, with Chekov and Spock as bystanders. Racially, the four made a colorful mixture, though probably none of them was aware of it.

". . . and I know from my actions you must all think me a volcanic hothead—erupting lava from my nostrils at danger signals that are only figments of my imagination. But believe me, my friends, there can be no moment when I can have my guard down where such as Bele are present. And so what happens? I act the madman out of the anger and frustration he forces upon me and thereby prove his point that I *am* a madman."

"We all act incorrectly when we're angry," Uhura said.

"After all," Chekov added cheerfully, "we're only human."

"Ah, Mr. Chekov, you have used the phrase which puts my impatience into perspective—which focuses on my lack of ability to convey to your captain, and to you, yes you here in this room, my lack of ability to alert you to the real threat of someone like Bele. There is no persecution on your planet. How can you understand my fear, my apprehension, my degradation, my suffering?"

"There was persecution on Earth once," Chekov said.

"Yes," said Uhura. "But to us, Chekov, that's only something we were taught in history class."

"Yes, that's right. It was long ago."

"Then," said Lokai, "how can I make your flesh know how it feels to see all those who are like you—and only because they are like you—despised, slaughtered and, even worse, denied the simplest bit of decency that is a living being's right. Do you know what it would be like to be dragged out of your hovel into a war on another planet? A battle that will serve your oppressor and bring death to you and your brothers?"

There seemed to be no answer to that.

Bele, for reasons not to be guessed at, continued to work on Kirk—perhaps because he had developed a grudging respect for the man who had faced him down, or perhaps not. He visited the Captain's quarters whenever asked, though Kirk took care on each occasion to see that Spock was present as well.

"Putting the matter in the hands of your Starfleet

Command is of course the proper procedure," Bele said on one such occasion. "Will it be long before we hear from them, Captain?"

"I expect the reply is already on the way, Commissioner."

"But Command may not arrive at the solution you anticipate," Spock added. "There is the matter of the shuttlecraft Lokai appropriated."

"Gentlemen," Bele said, almost airily, "we are discussing a matter of degree. Surely, stealing a shuttlecraft cannot be equated with the murder of thousands of people?"

"We don't know that Lokai has done that," Spock said.

"Well, the one thing we're agreed on is that Lokai is a criminal."

"We are agreed," Kirk said, "that he took a shuttlecraft—excuse me. Kirk here."

"Captain," Uhura's voice said, "I have your communication from Starfleet Command."

"Fine, Lieutenant. Read it out."

"Starfleet Command extends greetings to Commissioner Bele of the planet Cheron. His urgent request to be transported to his planet with the man he claims prisoner has been taken under serious consideration. It is with great regret that we report we cannot honor that request. Intragalactic treaty clearly specifies that no being can be extradited without due process. In view of the circumstances we have no doubt that after a hearing at Starbase, Commissioner Bele will be provided transportation, but whether with or without his prisoner remains to be determined. End of message."

Bele's face was a study in the attempt to retain a bland mask over anger. "As always," he said, "Lokai has managed to gain allies, even when they don't recognize themselves as such. He will evade, delay and escape again, and in the process put innocent beings at each other's throats—for a cause they have no stake in, but which he will force them to espouse violently by twisting their minds with his lies, his loathsome accusations, his foul threats."

"I assure you, Commissioner," Kirk said, "our minds will not be twisted by Lokai—or by you."

"And you're a leader of men—a judge of character?" Bele said contemptuously. "It is obvious to the most simpleminded that Lokai is of an inferior breed . . ."

"The evidence of our eyes, Commissioner," Spock said, "is that he is of the same breed as yourself."

"Are you blind, Commander Spock?"

"Obviously not; but I see no significance in which side of either of you is white. Perhaps the experience of my own planet may help you to see why. Vulcan was almost destroyed by the same conditions and characteristics that threaten to destroy Cheron. We were a people like you—wildly emotional, often committed to irrationally opposing points of view, to the point of death and destruction. Only the discipline of logic saved our people from self-extinction."

"I am delighted Vulcan was saved, Commander, but expecting Lokai and his kind to act with self-discipline is like expecting a planet to stop orbiting its sun."

"Maybe you're not a sun, and Lokai isn't a planet," Kirk said. "Give him a chance to state his grievances—listen to him—hear him out. Maybe he can change; maybe he *wants* to change."

"He cannot."

"Change is the essential process of all existence," Spock said. "For instance: The people of Cheron must have once been monocolored."

"Eh? You mean like both of you?"

"Yes, Commissioner," Kirk said. "There was a time—long ago, no doubt—when that must have been true."

Bele stared at them incredulously for a moment, and then burst into uproarious laughter.

While he was still recovering, the intercom sounded. "Scott here, Captain. We are orbiting Ariannus. We're ready with the decontamination procedure and Ariannus reports all ground precautions complete."

"Very good, Scotty, let her rip. Kirk out."

"I once heard," Bele said, still smiling, "that on some of your planets the people believe that they are descended from apes."

"Not quite," Spock said. "The apes are humanity's cousins, not their grandfathers. They evolved from common stock, in different directions. But in point of fact, all advanced forms of life have evolved from more primitive stages. Mutation produces changes, and the fittest of these survives. We have no reason to believe that we are at the end of the process—although no doubt the development of intelligence, which enables us to change our environment at will, has slowed down the action of selection."

"I am aware of the process," Bele said, somewhat ironically, "and I stand corrected on the detail. But I have told you that we are a very old race and a long-lived one. We have every reason to believe that we *are* the end of the process. The change is lost in antiquity, but it seems sensible to assume that creatures like Lokai, of generally low intelligence and virtually no moral fiber, represent an earlier stage."

"Lokai has sufficient intelligence to have evaded you for a thousand years," Kirk said. "And from what I've seen of you, that can't have been easy to do."

"Nevertheless, regardless of occasional clever individuals, whom we all applaud, his people are as I have described them. To suggest that behind both of us is a monochrome ancestor . . ."

The buzzer sounded again. "Captain, Scott here again. We have completed the decontamination orbit. Orders?"

"Program for Starbase 4. We'll be right with you."

Bele was showing signs of his strained and intense look of concentration which Kirk had no reason to recall with confidence. Kirk said, in the tone of an order, "Join us on the bridge, Commissioner?"

"Nothing I would like better."

But when they arrived, the bridge personnel were in turmoil. They were clustered around the computer, at which Scott was stationed.

"What's wrong?" Spock asked.

"I don't rightly know, Mr. Spock. I was trying to program for Starbase 4—as ordered—but I can't get a response."

Spock made a quick examination. "Captain, some of the memory banks are burned out."

"See if you can determine which ones."

"I will save you that trouble, Mr. Spock," Bele said. "They are in Directional Control and in the Self-Destruct circuit. You caught me by surprise with that Destruct procedure before." As he spoke, the fire sheath began to form around him. "Now can we go on to Cheron without any more discussion?"

"Stand clear of him," Kirk said. "Guard, shoot to stun."

The heat promptly increased. "I cannot block your weapon," Bele said, "but my heat shield will go out of control if I am rendered unconscious. This will destroy not only everyone here, but much of the ship's bridge itself."

The Cheronian was certainly a virtuoso at producing impasses. As he and Kirk glared at each other, the elevator doors parted and Lokai came storming out to the Captain.

"So this is the justice you promised after Ariannus! You have signed my death warrant! What do you do —carry justice on your tongues? Or will you fight and die for it?"

"After so many years of leading the fight," Kirk observed, "you seem very much alive."

"I doubt that the same can be said for many of his followers," Spock said.

Bele laughed contemptuously. At once, a fiery sheath grew also around Lokai.

"You're finished, Lokai. We've got your kind penned in their districts in Cheron. And they'll stay that way. You've combed the Galaxy and come up with nothing but monocolored primitives who snivel that they've outgrown fighting."

"I have given up on these useless pieces of bland flesh," Lokai raged. "But as for you, you—you half of a tyrant . . ."

"You image in a cheap mirror . . ."

They rushed together. Their heat shields fused into a single, almost solid mass as they struggled. Its edges drove the crew back, and wavered perilously near to the control boards.

"Bele!" Kirk shouted. "Keep this up and you'll never get to Cheron, you'll have wrecked the bridge! This will be your last battlefield—your thousand years of pursuit wasted!"

The combatants froze. Then Bele threw Lokai away from him, hard. Lokai promptly started back.

"And Lokai, you'll die here in space," Kirk continued.

"You'll inspire no more disciples. Your cause will be lost."

Lokai stopped. Then his heat shield went down, and so, a moment later, did Bele's.

"Captain," Spock said, "I believe I have found something which may influence the decision. I can myself compute with moderate rapidity when deprived of the machine . . ."

"Yes, and beat the machine at chess, too. Go on."

"Because of our first involuntary venture in the direction of Cheron, our orbit around Ariannus was not the one originally planned. I believe we can leave it for Starbase 4 in a curve which will pass us within scanning range of Cheron. With extreme magnification, we might get a visual readout. I can feed Mr. Sulu the coordinates; he will have to do the rest of the piloting by inspection, as it were, but after the piloting he did for us behind the Klingon lines* I am convinced he could fly his way out of the Cretan labyrinth if the need arose."

"I believe that too," Kirk said. "But what I don't see is what good you think will come out of the maneuver."

"Observing these strangers and their irreconcilable hatreds," Spock said, "has given me material to draw certain logical conclusions. At present it is only a hypothesis, but I think there would be value in testing it."

Anything Spock said was a possibly valid hypothesis was very likely to turn out to be what another man would have called a law of nature. Kirk said, "It is so ordered."

The visual readout of Cheron was wobbly, but growing clearer; Sulu had sufficiently improved upon Spock's rather indefinite course corrections so that the moment of closest approach would be not much over 15,000 miles. It was an Earthlike planet, but somewhat larger, by perhaps a thousand miles of diameter. Both Bele and Lokai were visibly moved by the sight. Well, a thousand years is a long time, Kirk thought, even for a long-lived race.

"There is your home, gentlemen," he said. "Not many details yet, but if you represent the opposing factions there typically, we must be picking up a raging battle."

"No, sir," Spock said from his console. The words

*See *Spock Must Die!*

could not have been simpler, but there was something in his tone—could it possibly have been sadness?—that riveted Kirk's attention, and that of the Cheronians as well. "No conflicts at all."

"What are you picking up?" Kirk said.

"Several very large cities. All uninhabited. Extensive traffic systems barren of traffic. Vegetation and lower animals encroaching on the cities. No sapient life forms registering at all, Captain."

"You mean the people are *all* dead?"

"Yes, Captain—all dead. This was what I had deduced when I suggested this course. They have annihilated each other—totally."

"My people," Bele said. "All dead."

"Yes, Commissioner," Spock said. "All of them."

"And—mine?" Lokai said.

"No one is left. No one."

The two survivors faced each other with ready rage.

"Your bands of murderers . . ."

"Your genocidal maniacs . . ."

"Gentlemen!" Kirk said in his command voice. Then, more softly, "The cause you fought for no longer exists. Give up your hate, and we welcome you to live with us."

Neither seemed to hear him; the exchange of glares went on.

"You have lost, Bele. I have won."

"You always think you win when you destroy."

"What's the matter with you two?" Kirk demanded, his own temper at last beginning to fray. "Didn't you hear my First Officer? Your planet is dead. Nobody is alive on Cheron just because of this kind of hate! Give it up, in heaven's name!"

"You have lost the planet," Lokai said. "I have won. I have won because I am free."

Suddenly, he made a tremendous leap for the elevator. The doors opened for him, and then, with a wild laugh, he was gone. Bele made as if to rush after him; Kirk stopped him.

"Bele—listen! The chase is finished."

"No, no! He must not escape me!"

"Where can he go?" Spock said.

"I think I know the answer to that," Uhura said. "Someone has just activated the Transporter."

"Oh," Kirk said. "Are we in Transporter range of Cheron?"

"Just coming into it," Spock said. "And a sentient life form is beginning to come through on the planet."

"It is he!" Bele cried. "Now I'll get him!"

He sprang for the elevator in turn. The guards, now belatedly alert, moved to stop him, but Kirk held up his hands.

"Let him go. Bele, there's no one there to punish him. His judges are dead."

"I," Bele said, "am his punisher." Then he too was gone.

There was a brief silence. Then Uhura said, "Captain, the Transporter has been activated again."

"Of course," Kirk said wearily. He felt utterly washed out. "Is he showing up on Cheron on the scanners now, Mr. Spock?"

"Some second sapient life form is registering. I see no other possible conclusion."

"But," Uhura said, "it doesn't make any sense."

"To expect sense from two mentalities of such extreme viewpoints is not logical," Spock said. "They are playing out the drama of which they have become the captives, just as their compatriots did."

"But their people are dead," Sulu said slowly. "How can it matter to them now which one is right?"

"It does to them," said Spock. "And at the same time, in a sense it does not. A thousand years of hating and running have become all of life."

"Spock," said McCoy's voice behind them, "may I remind you that I'm supposed to be the psychologist aboard this ship?"

"Spock's human half," Kirk said, turning, "is perhaps better equipped to perceive half measures taking over the whole man than the rest of us, Bones. And his Vulcan side quite accurately predicted the outcome. Hate wasn't all Lokai and Bele had at first, but by allowing it to run them, that's all they ended up with. This is their last battlefield—and let us hope that we never see its like again. Mr. Sulu, Warp Two for Starbase 4."

THIS SIDE OF PARADISE

(Nathan Butler and D. C. Fontana)

There was no answer from the Sandoval colony on Omicron Ceti III to the *Enterprise*'s signals, but that was hardly surprising; the colonists, all one hundred and fifty of them, had probably been dead for the better part of three years, as two previous colonies had died, for reasons then mysterious. Elias Sandoval had known this past history and had determined to settle on the planet anyhow; it was in all other respects a tempting place.

It was not until after his group had settled in—and had stopped communicating—that the Berthold emission of the planet's sun had been discovered. Little enough was known about Berthold radiation even now, but it had been shown that direct exposure to it under laboratory conditions distintegrated living animal tissue in as little as seventy-two hours. A planet's atmosphere would cut down some of the effect, to the point where a week's exposure might be safe, but certainly not three years. And there was no preventive, and no cure.

The settlement proper, however, was still there and was easy to spot. Kirk made up a landing party of six, including himself, Spock, McCoy, Lieutenant Timothy Fletcher (a biologist), Sulu and a crewman named

Dimont. The settlement proved to consist of a surprisingly small cluster of buildings, with fields beyond it. Kirk looked around.

"It took these people a year to make the trip from Earth," he said. "They came all that way—and died."

"Hardly that, sir," said a man's voice. The party snapped around toward it.

A big, bluff, genial-looking man clad in sturdy work clothes had come around a corner of a building, with two others behind him, similarly dressed and carrying tools. The first man came forward, holding out his hand.

"Welcome to Omicron Ceti III," he said. "I am Elias Sandoval."

Kirk took the hand, but could think of nothing to say but a mumble of thanks.

"We've seen no one outside our group since we left Earth four years ago," the man went on. "We've expected someone for quite some time. Our subspace radio has never worked properly and we, I'm afraid, had no one among us who could master its intricacies. But we were sure when we were not heard from, a ship would come."

"Actually, Mr. Sandoval, we didn't come because of your radio silence . . ."

"It makes little difference, Captain. You are here, and we are happy to have you. Come, let me show you our settlement."

He began to walk away, not bothering to look back, as if certain that they would follow. The other colonists had already left.

"On pure speculation," McCoy said drily, "just as an educated guess, I'd say that man isn't dead."

Spock checked his tricorder. "The intensity of Berthold radiation is at the predicted level. At this intensity, we will be safe for a week, if necessary. But . . ."

"But these people shouldn't be alive," Kirk said. "Well, there's no point in debating it in a vacuum. Let's get some answers."

He started after Sandoval. From closer range, the buildings could be seen to be not deserted, only quiet. Nearby, a woman was hanging out some wash; in another structure, a woman placed a fresh-baked pie in a window to cool. It might have been a tranquil Earthly farm community of centuries ago, except for a scattering of peculiar plants with bulbous pods, apparently indigenous, which revealed that it was on another planet.

Sandoval led the landing party into his own quarters. "There are two other settlements," he said, "but we have forty-five colonists here."

"What was the reason for the dispersal?" Kirk asked.

"We felt three separate groups might have a better opportunity for growth. And, if some disease should strike one group, the other two would be less likely to be endangered. Omicron is an ideal agricultural planet, Captain, and we determined that we would not suffer the fate of expeditions that had gone before us."

A woman came from an inner door and stopped, seeing the strangers. She looked Eurasian, and was strikingly beautiful.

"Ah, Leila," Sandoval said, turning to her. "Come and meet our guests. This is Leila Kalomi, our botanist. Captain Kirk, Dr. McCoy, Mr. Spock . . ."

"Mr. Spock and I have met," she said, holding out a hand to him. "It has been a long time."

He took the hand gently but awkwardly. "The years have seemed twice as long," he said.

She bowed her head, silently accepting the compliment. Then she looked up, as if searching his face for something more; but there was nothing but his usual calm. He released her hand slowly.

"Mr. Sandoval," Kirk said, "we do have a mission here. A number of examinations, tests . . ."

"By all means, please attend to them, Captain. I think you'll find our settlement interesting. Our philosophy is a simple one: that men should return to the less complicated life. We have very few mechanical things here—no vehicles, no weapons—" He smiled. "As I said, even the radio has never worked properly. We have harmony here—complete peace."

"We'll try not to disturb your work. Gentlemen, if you'll come outside now . . ."

On the porch, he flipped open his communicator. "Kirk to *Enterprise*."

"*Enterprise*. Lieutenant Uhura here."

"Lieutenant, we've found the colony apparently well and healthy. We're beginning an investigation. Relay that information to Starfleet, and then beam down to me all the information we have on this last Omicron expedition."

"Yes, sir. *Enterprise* out."

"Gentlemen, carry out your previous instructions. If you find anything out of the ordinary, report to me at once."

The party scattered.

Dimont was the first to find the next anomaly. He had been raised in the farm country of the Mojave, and was leading cows to pasture when he was six, up at dawn and then working all day in the fields. It was his opinion, expressed to Sulu, that "they could use a little of that spirit here."

But there was no place for it. There were no cows here; the one barn hadn't even been built for them, but only for storage. Nor were there any horses, pigs, even dogs. A broader check disclosed that the same was true of the whole planet: there was nothing on it but people and vegetation. The records showed that the expedition had carried some animals for breeding and food, but none seemed to have survived. Well, that was perhaps not an anomaly in the true sense, for they couldn't have survived. In theory, neither could the people.

But they had. "I've examined nine men so far," McCoy reported, "ages varying from twenty-three to fifty-nine. Every one of them is in perfect physical shape—textbook responses. If everybody was like them, I could throw away my shingle. But there's something even stranger."

"What is it?" Kirk asked.

"I've got Sandoval's medical record as of four years ago when he left Earth. There was scar tissue on his lungs from lobar penumonia suffered when he was a child. No major operations, but he did have an appendectomy. But when I examined the man not an hour ago, he was as perfect as the rest of them."

"Instrument malfunction?"

"No. I thought of that and tested it on myself. It accurately recorded my lack of tonsils and those two broken ribs I had once. But it *didn't* record any scar tissue on Sandoval's lungs—and it *did* record a healthy appendix where one was supposedly removed."

Fletcher's report also turned up an anomaly. "The soil here is rich, the rainfall moderate, the climate temperate the year round. You could grow anything here, and they've got a variety of crops in—grains, potatoes, beans. But for an agricultural colony they actually have very little acreage planted. There's enough to sustain the colony, but very little more. And another thing, they're not bothering to rotate crops in their fields—haven't for three years. That's poor practice for a group like this, even if the soil is good."

It was like a jigsaw puzzle all one color—a lot of pieces but no key to where they fitted.

Then came the order to evacuate, direct from Admiral Komack of Starfleet. Despite the apparent well-being of the colonists, they were to be moved immediately to Starbase 27, where arrangements were being made for complete examinations of all of them. Exposed Starship personnel were also to be held in quarantine until cleared at the Starbase. Apparently somebody up the line thought radiation disease was infectious. Well, with Berthold rays, anything seemed to be possible, as McCoy observed wrily.

"You'll have to inform your people of Starfleet's decision," Kirk told Sandoval. "Meanwhile we can begin to prepare accommodations for them aboard ship . . ."

"No," said Sandoval pleasantly.

"Mr. Sandoval, this is not an arbitrary decision on my part. It is a Starfleet order."

"This is completely unnecessary. We are in no danger here."

"We've explained the Berthold radiation and its effect," McCoy said. "Can't you understand . . ."

"How can I make *you* understand, Doctor? Your own instruments tell you we are in excellent health, and our records show we have not had one death among us."

"What about the animals?" Kirk said.

"We are vegetarians."

"That doesn't answer my question. Why did all the animals die?"

"Captain, you stress unimportant things," Sandoval said, as calmly as before. "We will not leave. Your arguments have some validity, but they do not apply to us."

"Sandoval, I've been ordered to evacuate this colony,

and that's exactly what I intend to do, with or without your help."

"And how will you do that?" Sandoval said, turning away. "With a butterfly net?"

It was Spock who was finally given the key. He was standing with Leila looking out over a small garden, checking his tricorder.

"Nothing," he said, "not even insects. Yet your plants grow, and you have survived exposure to Berthold radiation."

"It can be explained," Leila said.

"Please do."

"Later."

"I have never understood the female capacity to avoid a direct answer on any subject."

She put a hand on his arm. "And I never understood you, until now." She tapped his chest. "There was always a place in here where no one could come. There was only the face you allow people to see. Only one side you allow them to know."

"I would like to know how your people have managed to survive here."

"I missed you."

"You should be dead."

She took her hand from his arm and stepped back. "If I show you how we survived, will you try to understand how we feel about our life here? About each other?"

"Emotions are alien to me . . ."

"No. Someone else might believe that—your shipmates, your Captain. But not me. Come this way."

She led him to an open field, uncultivated, with pod plants growing amid grass and low brush. They rustled gently in a little breeze.

"This is the place," she said.

"It looks like any other such area. What is the nature of this thing, if you please?"

"The specific elements and properties are not important. What is important is that it gives life—peace—love."

"What you describe was once called in the vernacular 'a happiness pill.' And you, as a scientist, should know that is impossible."

"No. And I was one of the first to find them."

"Them?"

"The spores." She pointed to the pod plants.

Spock bent to examine them. At the same moment, one of the pods flew apart, like a powdery dandelion broken by the wind. Spock dropped his tricorder to shield his face as the powder flew up about him. Then he screamed.

Leila, frightened, moved forward a step, reaching out a hand to him.

"I—can't," he moaned, almost inaudibly. "Please—don't—don't . . ."

"It shouldn't hurt, not like this! It didn't hurt us!"

"I'm not—like you."

Then, slowly, his face began to change, becoming less rigid, more at peace. Seeing the change, Leila reached up to touch his cheek with gentle fingers. He reached out to gather her into his arms, very gently, as though afraid this woman and this feeling were so fragile that he might break them.

After the kiss, she sat down, and he lay down beside her, his head in her lap. "See the clouds," he said after a while. "That one looks like a dragon—you see the tail and the dorsal spines?"

"I have never seen a dragon."

"I have, on Berengaria VII. But I never saw one in a cloud before." His communicator abruptly shrilled, but he ignored it. "Or rainbows. Do you know I can tell you exactly why one appears in the sky—but considering its beauty was always out of the question."

"Not here," Leila said. The communicator shrilled again, insistently. "Perhaps you should answer?"

"It will only be the Captain."

But finally he lifted the communicator and snapped up the screen. Kirk's anxious voice sounded instantly. "Mr. Spock!"

"What do you want?" Spock asked lazily.

"Spock, is that you?"

"Yes, Captain. What do you want?"

"Where are you?"

Spock considered the question calmly. "I don't believe I want to tell you."

"Spock, I don't know what you think you're doing, but

this is an order. Report back to me at the settlement in ten minutes. We're evacuating the colony to Starbase 27 . . ."

"No, I don't think so."

"You don't think so *what?*"

"I don't think so, *sir.*"

"Spock, report to the settlement immediately. Acknowledge. Spock!"

The First Officer tossed the communicator away among the plants.

It seemed to be their fruiting time; they were bursting all over the area now. Fletcher was caught next, then McCoy, then Sulu and Dimont—and finally Kirk himself.

But Kirk alone was unaffected. As peace and love and tranquillity settled around him like a soggy blanket, he was blazing. His temper was not improved by the discovery that McCoy was arranging for transportation to the ship not of colonists or their effects, but of pod plants. Evidently a couple of hundred were already aboard. Hotter than ever, Kirk ordered himself to be beamed aboard.

He found the bridge deserted except for Uhura, who was busy at her communications board. All other instruments were on automatic.

"Lieutenant, put me through to Admiral Komack at Starfleet."

As she turned from the board, Kirk was shocked to see that she, too, wore the same sweet, placid expression as the others. She said, "Oh—I'm afraid I can't do that, Captain."

"I don't suppose," Kirk said tightly, "it would do any good to say that was an order."

"I know it was, Captain. But all communications are out."

"All?" Kirk reached past her and began to flick switches on the board.

"All except for ship to surface; we'll need that for a while. I short-circuited all the rest." She patted his arm. "It's really for the best."

She arose, and strolled away from him to the elevator, which swallowed her up. Kirk tried her board again, but to no effect. He slammed his fist down in aggravation.

Then he noticed a light pulsing steadily on Spock's library-computer. Moving to that station, he pushed the related button.

"Transporter Room."

There was no answer, but clearly the room was in use. He made for it in a hurry.

He found a line of crew personnel in the corridor leading to the Transporter Room. All waited patiently. Every so often the line moved forward a few steps.

"Report to your stations!"

The crewmen stared at him quietly, benevolently—almost pityingly.

"I'm sorry, sir," one of them said. "We're transporting down to join the colony."

"I said, get back to your stations."

"No, sir."

"Do you know what you're saying?"

"You've been down there," the crewman said earnestly. "You know how beautiful it is—how perfect. We're going."

"This is mutiny!"

"Yes, sir," the crewman said calmly. "It is."

Kirk went back to the bridge and to the communications board. As Uhura had said, ship to ground was still operative. He called McCoy, and was rather surprised to get an answer.

"Bones, the spores of your damnable plants have evidently been carried throughout the ship by the ventilation system. The crew is deserting to join the Omicron colony, and I can't stop them."

"Why, that's fine," McCoy said; his accent had moved considerably south of the Mason-Dixon line, almost to his Georgia boyhood. "Y'all come right down."

"Never mind that. At least you can give me some information. I haven't been affected. Why not?"

"You always were a stubborn cuss, Jimmy. But you'll see the light."

Kirk fumed in silence for a moment. "Can't you tell me anything about the physical-psychological aspects of this thing?"

"*I'm* not concerned with any physical-psychological aspects, Jim boy. We're all perfectly healthy."

"I've been hearing that word a lot lately. Perfect. Everything is perfect."

"Yup. That it is."

"I'll bet you've even grown your tonsils back."

"Uh-huh," McCoy said dreamily. "Jim, have you ever had a real, cold, Georgia-style mint julep?"

"Bones, Bones, I need your help. Can you run tests, blood samples, anything at all to give us some kind of lead on what these things are? How to counteract them?"

"Who wants to counteract Paradise, Jim?"

"Bones—" But the contact had been broken at the other end. Then he headed back for the Transporter Room. He was going to get some cooperation from his ship's surgeon if he had to take the madman by the ears.

He found Spock in Sandoval's office, both looking languidly pleased with themselves.

"Where's McCoy?"

"He said he was going to create something called a mint julep," Spock said, then added helpfully, "That's a drink."

"Captain," Sandoval said. "Listen to me. Why don't you join us?"

"In your own private paradise?"

Sandoval nodded. "The spores have made it that. You see, Captain, we *would* have died three years ago. We didn't know what was happening then, but the Berthold rays you spoke of affected us within two or three weeks of our landing here. We were sick and dying when Leila found the plants."

"The spores themselves are alien, Captain," Spock added. "They weren't on the planet when the other two expeditions were attempted. That's why the colonists died."

"How do you know all this?"

"The spores—tell us. They aren't really spores, but a kind of group organism made up of billions of submicroscopic cells. They act directly on the central nervous system."

"Where did they come from?"

"Impossible to tell. It was so long ago and so far away. Perhaps the planet does not even exist any longer. They drifted in space until finally drawn here by the Berthold radiation, on which they thrive. The plants are native, but they are only a repository for the spores until they find an animal host."

"What do they need us for?"

"Bodies. They do no harm. In return they give the host complete health and peace of mind . . ."

"Paradise, in short."

"Why not?" Spock said. "There is no want or need here. It's a true Eden. There is belonging—and love."

"No wants or needs? We weren't meant for that, any of us. A man stagnates and goes sour if he has no ambition, no desire to be more than he is."

"We have what we need," said Sandoval.

"Except a challenge! You haven't made an inch of progress here. You're not creating or learning, Sandoval. You're backsliding—rotting away in your paradise."

Spock shook his head sadly. "You don't understand. But you'll come around, sooner or later."

"Be damned to that. I'm going back to the ship."

He could not remember any time before when he had been so furious for so long a time.

The *Enterprise* was utterly deserted now. Without anybody aboard her, Kirk had a new and lonely realization of how big she was. And yet for all her immense resources, he was helpless. It was amazing how quickly all her entire complement had surrendered to the Lethe of the spores, leaving him and no one else raging futilely . . .

Raging?

Futilely?

Wait a minute.

There were pod plants all over the ship, so there was no problem about getting a sample. He took it down to McCoy's laboratory, located a slide, and then McCoy's microscope. A drop of water on the slide—right; now, mix some of the spores into the drop. Put the slide under the microscope. It had been decades since he had done anything like this, but he remembered from schooldays that one must run the objective lens down to the object, and then focus *up*, never down. Good; the spores came into register, tiny, and spined like pollen grains.

Getting up again, he went through McCoy's hypospray rack until he found one of a dozen all labeled *adrenaline*. He sprayed the slide, and then looked again.

There was nothing there. The spores were adrenalin-soluble. He had found the answer. It was almost incredibly dangerous, but there was no other way. He went back to the bridge and called Spock. If Spock didn't answer . . .

"Spock here. What is it now?"

"I've joined you," Kirk said quietly. "I understand now, Spock."

"That's wonderful, Captain. When will you beam down?"

"I've been packing some things, and I realized there's equipment aboard we should have down at the settlement. You know we can't come back aboard once the last of us has left."

"Do you want a party beamed up?"

"No, I think you and I can handle it. Why don't I beam you up now?"

"All right. Ready in ten minutes."

Kirk was waiting in the Transporter Room, necessarily, when the First Officer materialized, and was holding a metal bar in both hands, like a quarter-staff. Spock took a step toward him, smiling a greeting. Kirk did not smile back.

"*Now,*" he said harshly, "you mutinous, disloyal, computerized half-breed—we'll see about you deserting my ship!"

Spock stared. He seemed mildly surprised, but unflustered. "Your use of the term half-breed is perfectly applicable, Captain, but 'computerized' is inaccurate. A machine can be computerized, but not a man."

"What makes you think you're a man? You're an overgrown jackrabbit. You're an elf with an overactive thyroid."

"Captain, I don't understand . . ."

"Of course you don't! You don't have brains enough to understand! All you've got is printed circuits!"

"Captain, if you'll . . ."

"But what can you expect from a freak whose father was a computer and whose mother was an encyclopedia!"

"My mother," Spock said, his expression not quite so bland now, "was a teacher, my father an ambassador."

"He was a freak like his son! Ambassador from a planet

of freaks! The Vulcan never lived who had an ounce of integrity!"

"Captain—please—don't . . ."

"You're a traitor from a race of traitors! Disloyal to the core! Rotten—like all the rest of your subhuman race! And you've got the gall to make love to that girl! A human girl!"

"No more," Spock said stonily.

"I haven't even got started! Does she know what she's getting, Spock? A carcass full of memory banks that ought to be squatting on a mushroom instead of passing himself off as a man. You belong in a circus, Spock, not a starship! Right next to the dog-faced boy!"

With this, Kirk stepped forward and slapped the livid Spock twice, hard. With a roar, Spock swung out at him. Kirk leaped back out of his way, raising the bar of metal between his hands to parry the blow.

It was not much of a fight. Kirk was solely concerned with getting and keeping out of the way, while Spock was striking out with killing force, and with all the science of his once-warrior race. There could be only one ending. Kirk was deprived of the metal bar at the third onslaught, and finally took a backhand which knocked him to the floor against the far wall. Spock, his face contorted, snatched up a stool and lifted it over his head.

Kirk looked up at him and grinned ruefully. "All right, Mr. Spock. Had enough?"

Spock stared down at him, looking confused. Finally he lowered the chair.

"I never realized what it took to get under that thick hide of yours. Anyhow, I don't know what you're mad about. It isn't every First Officer who gets to belt his Captain—several times." He felt his jaw tenderly.

"You—you deliberately did that to me."

"Yes. The spores, Mr. Spock. Tell me about the spores."

Spock seemed to reach inside himself. "They're—gone. I don't belong any more."

"That was my intention. You said they were benevolent and peaceful. Violent emotions overwhelm and destroy them. I had to get you angry enough to shake off their influence. That's the answer, Spock."

"That may be correct, Captain, but we could hardly

initiate a brawl with over five hundred crewmen and colonists. It is not logical."

Kirk grinned. "I was thinking of something you told me once about certain subsonic frequencies affecting the emotions."

"Yes, Captain. A certain low organ tone induces a feeling of awe. There is another frequency that affects the digestion."

"None of those will do. I want one that irritates people—something that we could hook into the communications station and broadcast over the communicators."

"That would of course also have to involve a bypass signal." Spock thought a moment. "It can be done."

"Then let's get to work."

"Captain—striking a fellow officer is a court-martial offense."

"If we're both in the brig, who's going to build the subsonic transmitter?"

"That's quite logical, Captain. To work, then."

The signal generated by the modified Feinbergers and rebroadcast from the bypassed communicators went unheard in the settlement, but it was felt almost at once, almost as though the victims had had itching powder put under their skins. Within a few minutes, everyone's nerves were exacerbated; within a few more, fights were breaking out all over the colony. The fights did not last long; as the spores dissolved in the wash of adrenalin in the bloodstream, the tumult died back to an almost aghast silence. Not long after that, contrite calls began to come in aboard the *Enterprise*.

The rest was anticlimax. The crew came back, the colonists and their effects were loaded aboard, the plants were cleaned out of the ship except for one specimen that went to Lieutenant Fletcher's laboratory. Finally, Omicron Ceti III was dwindling rapidly on the main viewing screen, watched by Kirk, Spock and McCoy.

"That's the second time," McCoy said, nodding toward the screen, "that Man has been thrown out of Paradise."

"No—this time we walked away on our own. Maybe we don't belong in Paradise, Bones," Kirk said thoughtfully. "Maybe we're meant to fight our way through. Struggle. Claw our way up, fighting every inch of the way. Maybe we can't stroll to the music of lutes, Bones—we must march to the sound of drums."

"Poetry, Captain," Spock said. "Nonregulation."

"We haven't heard much from you about the Omicron Ceti III experience, Mr. Spock."

"I have little to say about it, Captain," Spock said, slowly and quietly, "except that—for the first time in my life—I was happy."

Both the others turned and looked at him; but there was nothing to be seen now but the Mr. Spock they had long known, controlled, efficient, and emotionless.

TURNABOUT INTRUDER

(Gene Roddenberry and Arthur H. Singer)

The *Enterprise* had been proceeding to a carefully timed rendezvous when she received a distress call from a group of archaeologists who had been exploring the ruins on Camus Two. Their situation was apparently desperate, and Kirk interrupted the mission to beam down to their assistance, together with Spock and McCoy.

In the group's headquarters they found two of the survivors, one of whom Kirk knew: Dr. Janice Lester, the leader of the expedition. She was lying on a cot, semiconscious. Her companion, Dr. Howard Coleman, looked healthy enough but rather insecure.

"What's wrong with her?" Kirk asked.

"Radiation sickness," said Coleman.

"I'd like to put the ship's complete medical facilities to work to save her. Can we get her aboard the *Enterprise*?"

"Exposing her to the shock of Transportation would be very dangerous. The radiation affects the nervous system."

McCoy looked up from his examination of the woman. "I can find no detectable signs of conventional radiation injury, Dr. Coleman," he said.

"Dr. Lester was farthest from the source. Fortunately for me, I was here at headquarters."

"Then the symptoms may not have completely developed."

"What happened to those who were closest to the point of exposure?" Kirk asked.

"They became delirious from the multiplying internal lesions and ran off mad with pain. They are probably dead."

"What form of radiation was it?" McCoy asked.

"Nothing I have ever encountered."

Janice Lester stirred and moaned, and her eyes fluttered open. Kirk came to her side and took her hand, smiling.

"You are to be absolutely quiet. Those are the doctor's orders, Janice, not mine."

Spock had been scanning with his tricorder. "Captain, I am picking up very faint life readings seven hundred meters from here. Help will have to be immediate."

Kirk turned to McCoy, who said, "There is nothing more to be done for her, Captain. Your presence should help quiet her."

As McCoy and Spock went out, Janice released Kirk's hand, and she said with great effort, "I hoped I would never see you again."

"I don't blame you."

Her eyes closed. "Why don't you kill me? It would be easy for you now. No one would know."

"I never wanted to hurt you," Kirk said, startled.

"You did."

"Only so I could survive as myself."

"I died. When you left me, I died."

"You still exaggerate," Kirk said, trying for the light touch. "I have heard reports of your work."

"Digging in the ruins of dead civilizations."

"You lead in your field."

She opened her eyes and stared directly into his. "The year we were together at Starfleet is the only time in my life I was alive."

"I didn't stop you from going on with space work."

"I had to! Where would it lead? Your world of Starship captains doesn't admit women."

"You've always blamed me for that," Kirk said.

"You accepted it."

"I couldn't have changed it," he pointed out.

"You believed they were right. I know you did."

"And you hated me for it. How you hated. Every minute we were together became an agony."

"It isn't fair . . ."

"No, it isn't. And I was the one you punished and tortured because of it."

"I loved you," she said. "We could have roamed among the stars."

"We would have killed each other."

"It might have been better."

"Why do you say that?" he demanded. "You're still young."

"A woman should not be alone."

"Don't you see now, we shouldn't be together? We never should have—I'm sorry. Forgive me. You must be quiet now."

"Yes." Her eyes closed and her head sank back on the cot.

"Janice—please let me help you this time."

In a deadly quiet voice, she said, "You are helping me, James."

He looked at her sadly for a moment and then turned away. The rest of the room, he noticed for the first time, was a litter of objects the group had collected from the ruins. The largest piece seemed to be an inscribed slab of metal, big enough to have been part of a wall. Kirk crossed to it. On its sides, he now saw, were what seemed to be control elements; some kind of machine, then. He wondered what sort of people had used it, and for what.

"A very remarkable object," Janice's voice said behind him.

"Really? What is it for, do you know?"

"Mentally superior people who were dying would exchange bodies with the physically strong. Immortality could be had by those who deserved it."

"And who chose the deserving?"

"In this case," she said, "I do."

The wall flared brilliantly in Kirk's face, and he felt a fearful internal wrench, as though something were trying to turn him inside out. When he could see again . . .

. . . he was looking at himself, through the eyes of Janice Lester.

Kirk/J left the wall, and coming over to the cot, found a scarf, which he began to fold. Then he bent and pressed it over the woman's mouth and nose.

"You had your chance, Captain Kirk. You could have smothered the life in me and they would have said Dr. Janice Lester died of radiation sickness acquired in the line of duty. Why didn't you? You've always wanted to!"

Janice/K's head moved feebly in denial. The scarf pressed down harder.

"You had the strength to carry it out. But you were afraid, always afraid. Now Janice Lester will take Captain Kirk's place. I already possess your physical strength. But *this* Captain Kirk is not afraid to kill." Kirk/J was almost crooning now, a song of self-hatred. "Now you know the indignity of being a woman. But you will not suffer long. For you the agony will soon pass—as it did for me."

The woman's hand tried to pull his away.

"Quiet. Believe me, it is better to be dead than to live alone in the body of a woman."

The struggling ceased, but Kirk/J did not release his hand until he heard footsteps outside. Then he replaced the scarf and went back to examining the wall. The search party entered only a moment later, looking grim.

"Your report, Dr. McCoy."

"We were too late. There was no way to help them."

"Was it radiation as reported?"

McCoy nodded. "I believe it was celebium. Dr. Coleman does not agree. It's essential to be specific."

"Why? Radioactivity is radioactivity, whatever the source."

"Yes, but in this case there was chemical poisoning involved as well. All the heavy elements are chemically virulent."

"Evidently," Spock added, "the field team broke through a newly exposed crust to a hidden cache of the radioactive element, whatever it was. The damage was instantaneous. They could not get away."

"That," Kirk/J said angrily, "will reflect on Dr. Lester's reputation for thorough preparedness."

"I don't think Dr. Lester can be blamed," McCoy said. "It was a most unfortunate accident, Captain."

"It was careless field work. Dr. Lester will be held responsible—unfair as it may be."

Dr. Coloman looked somewhat fearfully at Kirk/J and went quickly to Janice, bending to examine her. "Dr. McCoy!"

McCoy was there in an instant, tricorder out. "Jim, did you notice any unusual symptoms while we were gone?"

"Nothing at all. She has remained unconscious all the time."

"Dr. Lester is near death," Coleman said.

"Perhaps the shock of knowing what happened to her staff is part of the problem."

"I'm sure it is."

"Beaming her up to the *Enterprise,*" McCoy said, "would be less harmful than waiting."

Kirk/J looked questioningly at Coleman, who now seemed frightened. "I don't know," the man said.

"Then we'll go."

At Kirk/J's orders, two medical aides were ready with a stretcher when the party materialized in the Transporter Room. Coleman accompanied the patient to sickbay.

"Mr. Spock, take the ship out of orbit and resume designated course. Dr. McCoy, a word with you, please. You and Dr. Coleman disagree in your diagnosis. Please try to come to an agreement as fast as possible. The matter is especially disturbing—for personal reasons."

"I didn't realize you knew her so well," McCoy said.

"It has been a long time since I saw her. I walked out when it became serious."

"You must have been very young at the time."

"Youth doesn't excuse everything. It's a very unhappy memory."

"Everything possible will be done, Jim."

"Good. Thank you—Bones."

Kirk/J went to the bridge. Uhura, Chekov and Scott were all at their posts, as was Sulu. Spock was intent over his console. Kirk/J looked searchingly at the new faces, and Uhura and Sulu smiled back.

He came slowly to the Captain's position and touched the chair lightly, testing its maneuverability, almost as if with awe. Then he sat down in it and looked up at the viewing screen.

"Course, Mr. Chekov?"

"One twenty-seven, Mark eight."

"Mr. Sulu, set speed at Warp Factor Two."

"Warp Factor Two, sir."

"Mr. Spock, would you come here a moment, please? Thank you. We have a problem with our patient. The two doctors disagree on their diagnosis."

"That is hardly unusual in the medical fraternity, sir."

"Too bad it doesn't help cure their patients," Kirk/J said with an edgy smile.

"I think you can rely on Dr. McCoy's advice."

The edginess grew. "Do you have any specific evidence that confirms his opinion?"

"Not precisely, Captain. It is not my function."

"Then don't add to the confusion, Mr. Spock." Kirk/J arose and strode angrily to the elevator.

In sickbay, he found that Janice/K was regaining consciousness. Moments of quiet were interspersed with sudden flailing movements, which were restrained by straps, and moaning. A very frightened Dr. Coleman was pacing beside her.

"How long has this been going on?" Kirk/J asked.

"It just began."

"You must put a stop to it. If you let Dr. Lester become fully conscious, she will know what has happened."

"Probably no one will believe it," Coleman said.

"Probably?"

"That's all we can hope for. How could death be explained now?"

Kirk/J went to the head of the cot, Coleman following on the other side. "I tell you, it can't continue!"

"You killed every one of the staff. You sent them where you knew the celebium shielding was weak. Why didn't you kill *him?* You had the perfect opportunity."

"You didn't give me enough time."

"You had every minute you asked for."

"He hung onto life too hard. I couldn't . . ."

"You couldn't because you love him," Coleman said, his voice beginning to rise. "You want *me* to be his murderer."

"Love *him?*" Kirk/J said, his voice also rising. "I loved the life he led—the power of the Starship Commander. It's my life now."

"I won't become a murderer." Coleman turned and walked quickly toward the door. Kirk/J leaped to block his way.

"You *are* a murderer. You knew it was celebium. You could have treated them for that. You are a murderer many times."

The moaning grew louder. The doors to the medical lab opened and McCoy and Nurse Chapel came to the cot.

"I thought I could quiet Dr. Lester by my presence," Kirk/J said smoothly. "It seems to have had the opposite effect."

"It has nothing to do with you," Coleman said, with ill-concealed agitation. "It's a symptom of the developing radiation sickness."

"Tests with the ship's equipment," McCoy said, "show no sign of internal radiation damage."

"Dr. Coleman," Kirk/J said, "didn't Dr. Lester's staff become delirious before they went off to die?"

"Yes, Captain."

"But, Jim," said McCoy, "Dr. Lester could as easily be suffering from a phaser stun from all the symptoms I detect."

"Dr. Lester and her staff have been under my supervision for two years now," Coleman said stiffly. "If you do not accept my recommendations, responsibility for her health—or her death—will be yours."

Kirk/J looked toward the bed. Janice/K's movements were growing stronger. Then they stopped as her eyes opened; she looked about as if struggling to see and recognize the faces.

"Dr. McCoy," Kirk/J said, "I'm sorry, but I shall have to remove you from the case and turn it over to Dr. Coleman."

"You can't do that! On this ship, my medical authority is final."

"Dr. Coleman wishes to assume full responsibility. Let him do so."

"I will not allow it."

"It has been done." Kirk/J turned to Coleman. "Dr.

Lester is your patient. I believe you were about to administer a sedative when I came in."

"No!" the woman cried. "No sedative!" But the job was done.

Starting with the considerable advantage of her year in Starfleet with Kirk, Janice Lester had spent more years studying every single detail of a starship's operation—a knowledge which was now to be put to the test. With a little experience, she could probably become invulnerable to suspicion. But the presence aboard of the personality of James Kirk, even under sedation, was a constant threat to her position. It would be better to leave Janice/K among strangers, who would probably consider her insane.

"Plot a course for the Benecia Colony, Mr. Chekov. How long would it take to reach the colony at present speed?"

"Forty-eight hours, Captain."

"Captain," Spock said, "it will delay our work at Beta Aurigae. It means reversing course."

"It can't be helped. We must take Dr. Lester where she can be treated."

"May I point out, Captain, that Starbase Two is on the direct route to our destination?"

"How long to Starbase Two, Mr. Chekov?" Kirk/J asked.

"Seventy-two hours, sir."

"That's twenty-four hours too long. Dr. Lester's condition is increasingly serious. Continue present course."

"Captain, if the diagnosis of Dr. Lester's illness is the critical problem, the Benecia Colony is definitely not the place for her," Spock said. "Its medical facilities are the most primitive."

"They will have to serve the purpose."

"Starbase Two is fully equipped and staffed with the necessary specialists to determine exactly what is wrong with the Doctor. Isn't that crucial to your decision, Captain?"

"Thank you, Mr. Spock. But the facilities will be of no use if Dr. Lester is dead. Time is of the essence. Continue on course, Mr. Sulu."

"Captain," Uhura said, "shall I advise Starfleet Command of the change of plans?"

"No *change* of plan has been ordered, Lieutenant. Our arrival at Beta Aurigae will be *delayed*. Our gravitational studies of that binary system will not suffer, and we may save a life. That is not unusual procedure for the *Enterprise*." Kirk/J arose and went toward the elevator.

"I believe," Spock said, "Starfleet will have to know that our rendezvous with the Starship *Potemkin* will not be kept as scheduled."

"Mr. Spock—if you would concentrate on the areas for which you are responsible, Starfleet would have been informed already."

"Sir, the Captain deals directly with Starfleet on these matters. I assumed that action on my part would be deemed interference."

"Advise Starfleet of the delay, Lieutenant Uhura. Mr. Sulu, maintain course. Increase speed to Warp Six."

Kirk/J escaped from the bridge to the Captain's quarters, but there was no respite there; McCoy was waiting for him.

"Dr. McCoy, are we about to have another fruitless argument about diagnosis?"

McCoy's fist slammed on the top of Kirk's desk. "No, [illegible]—sir. I'll let my record speak for me."

"Why are you so defensive? There was no implied criticism of you in my order to remove you from the case."

"That's not why I'm here. I'm here because Dr. Coleman's record says he is incompetent."

"That's the opinion of an individual."

"No, sir. It's the considered opinion of Starfleet Command. I checked with them. Dr. Coleman was removed from his post as Chief Medical Officer of his ship for administrative incompetence . . ."

"Administrative duties are not required of him here."

"As well as for flagrant medical blunders."

"Promotions and demotions are sometimes politically motivated," Kirk/J said. "You know that, Doc."

"Not in Starfleet headquarters, *Captain*. At least, not in the Surgeon General's office."

Kirk/J paced for a moment. "I'm afraid the order will have to stand. Dr. Coleman's experience with what happened on the planet had to be the deciding factor. I'm sure you appreciate that."

"I appreciate that you had to make a decision. I, too, have that responsibility, Jim. So I'm asking you to report for a complete checkup."

"Why? What do you base it on?"

"Developing emotional instability and erratic behaviour since returning from the planet."

"You'll never make that charge stick!" Kirk/J said furiously. "Any fool can see why you're doing this!"

"Starfleet Command will be the judge of my motive."

"I won't submit to this petty search for revenge."

"You will submit to Starfleet regulations," McCoy said. "They state that the ship's surgeon will require a full examination of any member of the crew about whom he has doubts—including the Captain. I am ordering you to report for that examination . . ."

He was interrupted by the intercom buzzer.

"Captain Kirk here."

"Lieutenant Uhura, sir. Starfleet Command is requesting additional details of the delay. Shall I handle it?"

"I'll be right there."

The examination could not be postponed indefinitely, however. Knowledge of the Captain's aberrant behaviour was spreading throughout the ship; the crew was becoming increasingly tense. To McCoy's apparent surprise, however, Kirk/J satisfied every test completely.

This stroke of luck was followed by another. Struggling out from under sedation in Dr. Coleman's absence, Janice /K had avoided another injection by persuading Nurse Chapel of her docility—and then had sawed through her restraining straps with a broken medicine glass. Running wildly through the ship holding the glass like a weapon, calling for help and denouncing the Captain as a strutting pretender, she presented the perfect picture of a dangerous madwoman—giving Kirk/J all the pretext he needed to have her put in isolation in a detention cell, with around-the-clock security.

In this, however, he underestimated Spock, of whose sharp observation and penetrating logic the bogus Captain had had only the briefest of experience. The Science Officer knew the limitations of his discipline; he knew, in particular, that the essence of a man's being, his selfhood, was inherently impossible of access to any objective medical test—McCoy himself had often made just this point. Janice/K's denunciation planted a seed in his own mind.

Something had happened to the Captain while he was on the planet. Whatever it was could have taken place only in the short time while he was alone with Dr. Lester. A talk with her might be the only way to shed light on it.

There were two strapping guards outside her detention cell. Spock said to the first, "How is Dr. Lester?"

"Conscious and quiet, Mr. Spock."

"Good. I have a few questions to ask her."

"Did the Captain order it, sir?"

"Why should he?" Spock said. "They are my questions. Therefore I am ordering it, Ensign."

"But the Captain said no one was to speak to Dr. Lester."

"Has such an order ever included his senior officers?"

"Well, no, sir." The ensign activated the door and Spock started in. "But, Mr. Spock, I believe the Captain meant a guard was to be present."

"By all means."

Janice/K's first words on seeing them were "Thank God! Spock, you've got to listen to me."

"That is why I came," Spock said. "Apparently something happened while you and the Captain were alone. What was it?"

"She changed bodies with me, with the aid of an ancient machine she'd unearthed. Spock, *I am Captain Kirk.* I know how unbelievable it sounds. But that's how it happened."

"It is a possibility I had not considered."

"Unless I can convince you, I have no hope at all of ever getting out of this body."

"Complete life-entity transfer with the aid of a mechanical device?"

"Yes. Dr. Lester's description of its function is the last moment I remember as myself."

"To my knowledge," Spock said, "such total transfer has never been accomplished with complete success anywhere in the Galaxy."

"It was accomplished and forgotten long ago on Camus II. I am a living example."

"That is your claim. As yet, it is unsubstantiated."

"I know, Spock. Nevertheless I'm speaking the truth. Listen—when I was caught in the interspace of the Tholian sector, you risked your life and even the *Enterprise* to get me back. Help me get back now. And, when the Vians of Minara demanded that we let McCoy die, we didn't permit it. How would I know those things if I were not James Kirk?"

"Such incidents may have been recorded. They could have become known to you."

"You are closer to the Captain than anyone in the universe. You know his thoughts. What does your telepathic sense tell you?"

Spock touched her face and closed his eyes, his own face a study in concentration as he established a mind meld. Then he withdrew his hand and looked at her with new determination.

"I believe you," he said. "My belief is not acceptable evidence. But I will make every effort to make it so. Only Dr. McCoy can help us. Come with me."

"I'm sorry, sir," the guard said. "But Dr. Lester can *not* leave here. You're asking me to violate the Captain's order."

"He is not the Captain."

"Sir, you must be as mad as she is. You're to leave here at once. I follow orders."

"Certainly, Ensign," Spock said. "We must all do our duty."

While he was still talking, he lashed out. The scuffle was brief, but the guard outside the cell was alert—he could be heard calling, "Security to Captain Kirk! The detention cell has been broken into!"

When they emerged, the guard was standing with his back to the opposite wall, phaser leveled. Kirk/J and two more guards were already coming down the corridor, followed by McCoy.

Spock stopped. "Violence is not called for, sir," he said. "No *physical* resistance will be offered."

Kirk/J hit the intercom button. "Security detail to Detention at once. Attention all personnel. First Officer Spock is being placed under arrest on a charge of mutiny. He has conspired with Dr. Lester to take over the ship from your Captain. A hearing will be immediately convened to consider the charges and specifications for a general court-martial." He turned to McCoy. "The board will consist of Scott, you and myself."

"I will not be made party to a court-martial of Spock," McCoy said. "There are better ways to handle it."

"You are not forced to condemn anyone. You are asked —no, you are ordered—to vote your honest convictions. Two out of three carries the final verdict. Convene the board. Guard, return Dr. Lester to isolation. She will be held for sanity tests."

The hearing was held in the briefing room. Kirk/J sat at the head of the table, gavel in hand; McCoy sat quietly to one side. Uhura was making a tape of the proceedings, and Chekov, Sulu and Nurse Chapel were listening intently as Scott began cross-examining Spock.

"Mr. Spock, you are a scientist—a leading scientist of the Galaxy."

"That's very pleasant to hear, Mr. Scott. But it is an exaggeration. I have long since sacrificed basic theoretical investigation for the more immediate excitement of life on the *Enterprise*."

"I meant, your approach to every problem is completely scientific."

"I hope so," Spock said.

"Therefore your statement that you believe this fantastic tale about transference of life entities between the Captain and Dr. Lester is intended to be taken seriously by this court."

"Completely seriously."

"Yet you have no evidence on which to base it."

"I have stated my evidence: telepathic communication with the mind of Captain James T. Kirk."

"You are a reasonable man, Spock," Scott said, exasperated. "But that is not a reasonable statement. Far from it. Far from it. Surely you must have had more than that to go on."

"It was sufficient for me."

"Well, it's not sufficient for a court. Your evidence is completely subjective. You know that, laddie. What has happened to you? We must have evidence we can examine out in the open."

Spock threw a challenging look toward Kirk/J. "You have heard a great deal of testimony—except that of the chief witness. The one who should be the real subject of this inquiry is kept locked away in isolation. Why, *Captain*?"

"She is dangerously insane," Kirk/J said. "We have seen evidence of that."

"She is dangerous only to your authority, *sir*."

"Mr. Spock, my authority was granted to me by Starfleet Command. Only that high authority can take it away."

"Then why be afraid of the testimony of a poor insane woman?"

"This clumsy effort does not threaten my position, Mr. Spock. It does endanger your whole future."

"The witness, sir! Bring on the witness! Let your officers put the questions!"

Kirk/J hesitated a moment. Then he banged his gavel and nodded to a guard, who went out.

"Dr. McCoy."

"Yes, Captain."

"You were at one time disturbed by my orders and reactions, is that not true?"

"Yes, sir."

"But instead of trying to destroy me, you were searching for a way to help me. For the record, tell the court your findings."

"Physically the Captain is in the best of condition. His emotional and mental states are comparable to the time he assumed command of the *Enterprise*."

"Mr. Spock, did you know the results of Dr. McCoy's examination?"

"I know them now," Spock said.

"And what have you to say now?"

"I am disappointed and deeply concerned that there is no objective evidence to support my position—so far."

"Since there is no evidence, will you give up your belief in the insane story of a woman driven mad by a tragic experience?"

Before Spock could reply, the door opened and the woman in question herself was brought in by two guards. Kirk/J pointed to a chair, and she sat down.

"Dr. Lester," he said, "I appreciate your being here. Everyone is deeply aware that you have already been subjected to inordinate emotional stress. Unfortunately, I have had to add to it in the interest of the safety of this crew. I had hoped that any further stress could be avoided. Mr. Spock disagrees. He is of the opinion that your testimony is important in determining the merits of his case. Since we are solely interested in arriving at a just decision, we must ask you a few questions. We shall all try not to upset you." At this, she nodded. "Now. You claim you are James T. Kirk."

"No, I am not Captain Kirk," Janice/K said composedly. "That is very apparent. I doubt that Mr. Spock would have put it that way. I claim that whatever it is that makes James Kirk a living being special to himself is held here in this body."

"I stand corrected. However—as I understand it—I am Dr. Janice Lester."

There was a snicker from the guards.

"That's very clever," she responded. "But I didn't say it. I said the body of James Kirk is being used by Dr. Janice Lester."

"A subtle difference that happens to escape me," Kirk/J said with a smile. "However, I assume that this—this switch was brought about by mutual agreement."

"No. It was brought about by a violent attack by Dr. Lester, with the use of equipment she discovered on Camus II."

"Violence by the lady perpetrated on Captain Kirk? Tsk, tsk. I ask the assembled personnel to look at Dr. Lester and visualize that historic moment."

This time the laughter was general. Kirk/J waited until it had ridden itself out, then continued, "And do you know any reason why Dr. Janice Lester would want this ludicrous exchange?"

"Yes! To achieve a power her peers would not accord her. To attain a position she does not merit by training or temperament. And most of all she wanted to murder the man who might have loved her—had her intense hatred of her own womanhood not made life with her impossible."

Spock rose angrily. "Sir, this line of questioning is self-serving. There is only one issue: Is the story of life-entity transfer believable? This crew has been to many places in the Galaxy. *You have not*. They are familiar with many strange events. They are trained to recognize that what seems completely unbelievable on the surface is scientifically possible if you understand the basic theory of the event."

"Mr. Spock, do you know of any other case like the one Dr. Lester describes?"

"Not precisely. No."

"Assuming you are correct in your belief, do you expect Starfleet Command to place that person"—his finger stabbed at Janice/K—"in command of this ship?"

"I expect only to reveal the truth."

"Of course you do. And with the truth revealed that I am not really the Captain—and knowing that she will not be appointed Captain—then of course *you* will become the Captain." Kirk/J looked at Spock with apparent compassion. "Give it up, Spock. Return to the *Enterprise* family. All charges will be dropped. The madness that temporarily overcame us all on Camus II will pass and be forgotten."

"And what will happen to Dr. Lester?"

"Dr. Lester will be properly cared for. Always. That is a debt and a responsibility I owe her from the past."

"No, sir!" Spock said emphatically. "I will not withdraw a single charge I have made. You are not Captain Kirk. You have ruthlessly appropriated his body. But the life entity within you is not that of Captain Kirk. You do not belong in command of the *Enterprise*. I will do everything in my power against you."

"Lieutenant Uhura," Kirk/J said with dangerous quietness, "play back the last two sentences of Mr. Spock's tirade."

Spock's voice rang out from the speaker of the recorder: "You do not belong in command of the *Enterprise*. I will do everything in my power against you."

"Mr. Spock, you have heard the statement you put into the record. Do you understand the nature of it?"

"I do. And I stand by it."

"And that is mutiny!" Kirk/J shouted, his face livid. "Deliberate—vindictive—insane at its base—but it is mutiny as charged and incitement to mutiny. Dr. McCoy, Mr. Scott, you have heard it. On the basis of these statements, I call for an immediate summary court-martial by powers granted to me as Captain of the *Enterprise*."

"Just a moment, Captain," Scott said. "I'm not ready to

vote Mr. Spock into oblivion so fast. Mr. Spook is a serious man. What he says is to be taken seriously, no matter how wild."

"Come to the point."

"I'm right at the nub of it, Captain. You don't put a man like Mr. Spock out of the service because of a condition akin to temporary insanity. Dr. McCoy, you said the woman may have become mentally deranged due to the radiation she was exposed to."

"Yes, Scotty."

"Couldn't the same thing have happened to Mr. Spock? He was a sight closer to the source of the radiation."

"It's possible."

"Then the mutiny is qualified by the temporary insanity due to the . . ."

"Thank you, my friend," Spock interrupted. "A noble try. But I was not exposed to the colcbium. I took every precaution. And I have been given precautionary treatment since then by Dr. McCoy. I am completely sound in body and mind."

"Mutiny," said Kirk/J, pounding with the gavel. "A summary court-martial on the evidence and the charges is immediately invoked. A recess will be followed by a vote."

"Yes," Spock said. "An immediate vote. This matter must be cleared up at once, before . . ."

The gavel pounded a loud tattoo. "Silence!"

"Before our chief witness," Spock shouted above the din, "is left to die on an obscure little colony with the truth locked away inside her!"

Kirk/J rose, his face red with hysteria, almost to the point of apoplexy. "Silence, silence! A recess is declared. The summary court will then be in session. There will be no cross-discussion. No conferences. No collusion. I order the judges to be absolutely silent as they arrive at a decision on the charge of mutiny. When I return we will vote. The evidence presented here can be the only basis for your decision."

He stormed out of the room, leaving everyone stunned. McCoy began to pace. The silence stretched out. At last Scott said, "Who ever heard of a jury being forbidden to deliberate?"

He went out into the corridor, followed by the others,

leaving behind Janice/K, Spock and the guards, as well as Uhura.

"What's there to say?" McCoy said.

"Doctor, I've seen the Captain feverish, sick, drunk, delirious, terrified, overjoyed, boiling mad. Until now I've never seen him beet-red with hysteria. I know how I'm going to vote."

"I've been through this with Spock. He is not being scientific. And neither are you."

"It may not be scientific," Scott said, "but if Spock thinks it happened, it must be logical."

"Don't you think I know that? My tests show nothing wrong with the Captain. That's the only fact that will interest Starfleet."

"Headquarters has its problems—and we've got ours. Right now the Captain of the *Enterprise* is our problem."

McCoy frowned. He started to pace again, but was halted by Nurse Chapel.

"Doctor," she said, whispering, "I didn't notice it at the time. But in her first lucid moment, Dr. Lester asked why we were going to miss our rendezvous with the *Potemkin*. How could she know that?"

"Hmm. Especially since the Captain *didn't*. Scotty, the vote is going to be called in a few minutes."

"Let me put one last question. Suppose you voted with me in favor of Spock. That's two to one and Spock is free. What do you think the Captain will do?"

"I don't know."

"You know, all right. The vote will stick in his craw. He'll never accept it."

McCoy angrily walked away a few steps and then turned back and looked hard at Scott. "We don't know that."

"I tell you, he won't. Then, Doctor, that's the time to move against him. We'll have to take over the ship."

"We're talking mutiny, Scotty."

"Yes. Are you ready for the vote?"

"I'm ready for the vote."

Kirk/J was already back in the briefing room when they reentered. When they were all seated, he stood up. "Lieutenant Uhura, play back the tapes of the conversation in the corridor."

Uhura, looking both grief-stricken and guilt-ridden, moved a switch. Recorded voices said:

"Then, Doctor, that's the time to move against him. We'll have to take over the ship."

"We're talking mutiny, Scotty."

"Yes. Are you ready for the vote?"

"That's enough," McCoy said angrily. "We know what was said."

"Enough to convict you for conspiracy with mutineers," Kirk/J said, drawing his phaser. The guards followed suit. "You are so charged. The penalty is death."

Chekov and Sulu both jumped forward, talking almost at once.

"Starfleet expressly forbids the death penalty . . ."

"There is only one exception . . ."

"General Order Four has not been violated by any officer of the *Enterprise* . . ."

"All my senior officers have turned against me," Kirk/J said. "I am responsible. Execution will be immediate. Go to your posts. Guards, take them to the brig."

Only Uhura, Sulu and Chekov were at their posts on the bridge, a sadly depleted corporal's guard. They were working, but their expressions were listless, abstracted. Sulu said at last, "The Captain really must be cracking up if he thinks he can get away with an execution."

"Captain Kirk wouldn't order an execution even if he did crack up," Chekov said. "Spock's right, that can't be the Captain."

"What difference does it make who he is?" said Uhura. "Are we going to allow an execution to take place?"

Chekov clenched his fists. "If Security backs him up, how will we fight them?"

Sulu said, "I'll fight them every way and any way I can . . ."

The conversation was choked off as Kirk/J came onto the bridge, highly elated. When he spoke, the sentences seemed almost to tumble over one another in their haste to get out. "Lieutenant Uhura, inform all sections of the decision. Have each section send a representative to the place of execution on the hangar deck. Mr. Chekov, how far to the Beneccia Colony?"

"Coming within scanning range."

"Plot coordinates for orbit. Mr. Sulu, lock into coordinates as soon as orbit is accomplished. Interment will take place on Benecia."

There were no "Ayes," and nobody moved. Kirk/J stared at his officers. "You have received your orders."

Still no response.

"You have received your orders. You will obey at once or be charged with mutiny." His voice began to rise in pitch, losing its male timbre. "Obey my orders or—or . . ."

Then, suddenly, he reeled, staggered, and fell into his chair, seemingly almost in a faint. His body contorted for a moment and then became rigid, his eyes staring wider, but sightlessly.

The others rose in alarm, but the seizure lasted only a moment. Then Kirk/J was out of the chair and leaped for the elevator.

Dr. Coleman was alone in the medical lab when Kirk/J burst in. "Coleman—the transference is weakening."

"What happened?"

"For a moment I was with the prisoners. I won't go back to being Janice Lester. Help me prevent it."

"The only way to prevent it is by the death of Janice Lester. You'll have to carry out the execution."

"I can't," Kirk/J said. "The crew is in mutiny. You must kill him for me."

"I have done everything else for you. But I tell you I will not commit murder for you."

"You can do it for yourself," Kirk/J said urgently. "If I am the Captain of the *Enterprise*, you will regain your position as a Ship's Surgeon. I will see to that."

"I would have been content with you, as you were. I did not need a starship."

"Unless Kirk dies, we will both be exposed as murderers. Does that leave you any choice?"

Reluctantly, Coleman picked up an air hypo, selected a cartridge and snapped it into place.

"The dose must be doubly lethal."

"It is," Coleman said impassively.

Kirk/J led the way to the brig. Judging by the woman's tense expression and the way the others were grouped around her, she too had felt that moment of transitory retransference, and was ready to fight to prolong it should it occur again.

"I have demanded the sentence of execution," Kirk/J said. "However, to prevent any further conspiracy, you will be placed in separate cells. If there is any resistance, a sedative will be administered until you learn cooperation. Dr. Lester is first. Follow Dr. Coleman."

Coleman went back out through the force field. Janice/K held back suspiciously, but then also stepped out into the corridor, Kirk/J behind her. After only a few steps he said loudly, "This woman obviously doesn't know what it means to obey an order."

The hypo flashed in Coleman's hand, but not quickly enough. Janice/K saw it and grabbed that arm with both hands, struggling with all her poor strength to deflect it.

Again the look of dizziness and complete terror overwhelmed Kirk/J; once more his body contorted and grew taut.

The same paralysis gripped Janice/K, its rigidity immobilizing Coleman's arm as her conscious efforts could never have done. Then she screamed.

"Don't! Don't! I have lost to the Captain! I have lost to James Kirk!" And then, in a cry of pure madness, "Kill him! Kill *him!*"

Kirk, whose first move had been to shut off the brig's force field, met Coleman's rush easily; a quick chop and it was over. He turned to Janice, whose face was contorted with hatred and agony. "Kill him! I want James Kirk dead! Kill him!" Then, sobbing painfully like a child, "I will never be the Captain—never—never—kill him . . ."

Coleman, who had been only momentarily stunned, tossed aside the hypo, clambered to his feet and came over to her. She began to collapse, and Coleman took her in his arms.

"You are," he said, "as I have loved you."

"Kill him," Janice said quietly, her eyes vacant. "Please."

Spock, McCoy and Scott were all out in the corridor. Kirk seized each of them in turn by the hand. "Bones, is there anything you can do for her?"

"I would like to take care of her," Coleman said pleadingly.

"Of course," said McCoy. "Come with me." He led them away toward sickbay.

Kirk looked after them. "I didn't want to destroy her," he said.

"You had to," Spock said. "How else could you have survived, Captain? To say nothing of the rest of us."

"Her life could have been as rich as any woman's, if only—" He paused and sighed. "If only . . ."

"If only," Spock said, "she had ever been able to take any pride in *being* a woman."

REQUIEM FOR METHUSELAH

(Jerome Bixby)

Rigellian fever struck aboard the *Enterprise* with startling suddenness, its origin unknown. Permission was asked, and received, of Starfleet Command to abort the current routine mission in order to search for a planet with large deposits of ryetalyn, the only known cure for the disease. By the time they found such a planet, one yeoman had died and four more were seriously ill.

Kirk, McCoy and Spock beamed down at once, leaving Scott at the con. McCoy scanned about him with his tricorder.

"There's a large deposit at bearing two seven three—about a mile away," he reported, his voice grim. "We've got four hours to get it processed, or the epidemic will be irreversible. Everybody on the *Enterprise* . . ."

As he started off with Kirk, Spock's voice stopped them.

"Most strange," he said. "Readings indicate a life form in the vicinity. Yet our ship's sensors indicated that this planet was uninhabited."

"Human?" Kirk said. "But we've got no time for that. Let's get to that ryetalyn deposit."

Again they started off, and again they were halted by a

sound—this time a steady whirring behind them. As they turned, they saw floating from behind a rock what could only be a robot: metallic, spherical, about the size of a beachball, studded with protuberances with functions which could only be guessed at. It came toward them at about chest height, flickering menacingly.

The three drew their phasers. A light blinked brightly on the robot's skin, and a bush next to Kirk went up in a burst of flame.

First Kirk and then the other two fired back—or tried to. All three phasers were inoperative. The robot continued to advance.

"Do not kill," a man's voice said. The robot stopped in midair. The owner of the voice came around from behind the same rock: a muscular man of about forty, whose bearing suggested immense dignity, assurance, authority.

"Thanks," said Kirk with relief. "I am Captain James Kirk, of the . . ."

"I know who you are. I have monitored your ship since it entered this system."

"Then you know why we're here, Mr. . . . ."

"Flint. You will leave my planet."

"*Your* planet, sir?" Spock said.

"My retreat—from the unpleasantness of life on Earth—and the company of other people."

"Mr. Flint, I've got a sick crew up there," Kirk said. "We can't possibly reach another planet in time. We're sorry to intrude. We'll be happy to leave your little private world as soon as possible, but without that ryetalyn, you'd be condemning four hundred and thirty people to death!"

"You are trespassing, Captain."

"We're in *need*. We'll pay you for the ryetalyn—trade for it—work for it."

"You have nothing I want," Flint said.

"Nevertheless, we've got to have the ryetalyn. If necessary, we'll take it."

"If you do not leave voluntarily, I have the power to force you to leave—or kill you where you stand."

Kirk whipped out his communicator and snapped it open. "Kirk to *Enterprise*. Mr. Scott, lock phasers on landing party coordinates."

"Aye, Captain. All phasers locked on."

"If anything happens to us, there'll be *four* deaths," Kirk told Flint. "And my crew will come down and get the ryetalyn anyhow."

"It would be an interesting test of power," Flint said. "Your enormous forces—against mine. Who would win?"

"If you are not certain," Spock said, "I suggest you refrain from a most useless experiment."

"We need only a few hours," Kirk added.

"Have you ever seen a victim of Rigellian fever?" McCoy said. "It kills in one day. Its effects resemble bubonic plague."

Flint's expression turned remote. "Constantinople, Summer, 1334. It marched through the streets—the sewers. It left the city, by oxcart, by sea—to kill half of Europe. The rats—rustling and squealing in the night, as they, too, died . . ."

"You are a student of history, Mr. Flint?" Spock asked.

"I am." He seemed to rouse himself. "The *Enterprise*—a plague ship. Well, you have two hours. At the end of that time, you will leave."

"With all due gratitude," Kirk said, rather drily. "Mr. Spock, Bones . . ."

"No need," Flint said, indicating the robot. "M-4 will gather the ryetalyn you need. In the meantime, permit me to offer more comfortable surroundings."

"More comfortable" turned out to be a vast understatement. The central room of Flint's underground home was both huge and luxurious. Most impressive were the artworks—framed paintings, dozens of them, hung on the walls, except for one wall which was entirely taken up by books. There were statuary, busts, tapestries, illuminated glass cases containing open books and manuscripts of obvious antiquity, and even a concert grand piano. The place was warm, comfortable, masculine despite all these riches—at once both museum and home.

"Our ship's sensors did not reveal your presence here, Mr. Flint," Spock said.

"My planet is surrounded by screens which create the impression of lifelessness. A protection against the curious—the uninvited."

"Such a home must be difficult to maintain."

"M-4 serves as butler, housekeeper, gardener—and guardian."

McCoy was looking into the illuminated cases with obvious awe. "A Shakespeare First Folio—a Gutenberg Bible—the 'Creation' lithographs by Taranullus of Centaurus VII—some of the rarest books in the Galaxy—spanning centuries!"

"Make yourselves comfortable," Flint said. "Help yourselves to some brandy, gentlemen." He went out, calmly.

"Do we trust him?" McCoy asked.

"It would seem logical to do so—for the moment."

"I'll need two hours," McCoy said worriedly, "to process that ryetalyn into antitoxin."

"If the ryetalyn doesn't show up in one hour, we go prospecting," Kirk said. "Right over Mr. Flint, if necessary."

Spock was now looking at the paintings. "This is the most splendid private art collection I have ever seen," he said. "And unique. The majority are works of three men: Leonardo da Vinci of the sixteenth century, Reginald Pollock of the twentieth century, and even a Sten from Marcus II."

"And this," said McCoy, going over to the bar and picking up a bottle, "is Sirian brandy, a hundred years old. Now where are the glasses? Ah. Jim? I know you won't have any, Spock. Heaven forbid that your mathematically perfect brainwaves be corrupted by this all too human vice."

"Thank you, Doctor. I will have brandy."

"Can the two of us handle a drunk Vulcan?" McCoy asked Kirk. "Once alcohol hits that green blood . . ."

"Nothing happens that I cannot control much more efficiently than you," Spock said, after a sip. "If I appear distracted, it is because of what I have seen. I am close to feeling an unaccustomed emotion."

"Let's drink to *that*," McCoy said. "What emotion?"

"Envy. None of these da Vinci paintings has ever been catalogued or reproduced. They are *unknown* works. All are apparently authentic—to the last brushstroke and use of materials. As undiscovered da Vincis, they would be priceless."

"Would be?" Kirk said. "You think they might be fakes?"

"Most strange. A man of Flint's obvious wealth and impeccable taste would scarcely hang fakes. Yet my tricorder analysis indicates that the canvas and the pigments used are of contemporary origin."

"This could be what it seems to be," Kirk said thoughtfully. "Or it could be a cover—a setup—even an illusion."

"That could explain the paintings," McCoy said. "*Similar* to the real thing . . ."

"One of you, get a full tricorder scan of our host," Kirk said. "See if he's human."

"The minute he turns his back," McCoy agreed.

Kirk got out his communicator. "Kirk to *Enterprise*. Mr. Scott, run a library check on this Mr. Flint we've encountered here—and on this planet, Holberg 917-G. Stand by with results; I'll contact."

"Aye, sir."

"Kirk out. Now let's enjoy his brandy. It *tastes* real."

But as he lifted the glass to his lips, he once again heard the whirring of the robot, M-4. The men froze warily as the machine entered and moved toward them, stopping to hover over a large, low table. A front panel opened, and out came cubes of a whitish material onto the table. The robot closed the panel and floated back a pace.

McCoy snatched up one of the cubes. "This looks like—it is! Ryetalyn! Refined—ready to be processed into antitoxin!"

"Whatever our host may be, he's come through," Kirk said. "McCoy, beam up to the ship and start processing."

"That will not be necessary," Flint said, appearing at the top of a ramp. "M-4 can prepare the ryetalyn for inoculation more quickly in my laboratory than you could aboard your ship."

"I'd like to supervise that, of course," McCoy said.

"And when you are satisfied as to procedures, I hope you will do me the honor of being my guests at dinner."

"Thank you, Mr. Flint," Kirk said. "I'm afraid we don't have time."

Flint came a step down the ramp. "I regret my earlier inhospitality. Let me make amends." He half turned, extending a hand.

At the top of the ramp appeared a staggeringly beautiful girl in loosely flowing robes. She looked down at the three strangers with a mixture of innocence and awe.

The two descended the ramp. The girl was graceful as well as lovely, yet she seemed quite unaware of the charm she radiated.

"I thought you lived alone, Mr. Flint," Kirk said when he could get his voice back.

"No, this is the other member of the family. Gentlemen, may I present Rayna."

The courtesies were exchanged. Then Rayna said, "Mr. Spock, I do hope we can find time to discuss inter-universal field densities, and their relationship to gravity vortex phenomena."

If Spock was as staggered as Kirk was by this speech, he did not show it. "Indeed? I should enjoy such a talk. It is an interest of mine."

"Her parents were killed in an accident, while in my employ," Flint explained. "Before dying, they placed their infant, Rayna Kapec, in my custody. I have raised and educated her."

"With impressive results, sir," McCoy said. "Rayna, what else interests you besides gravity vortex phenomena?"

"Everything. Less than that is betrayal of the intellect."

"The totality of the universe?" McCoy said gently. "All knowledge? Remember, there's more to life than knowing."

"Rayna possesses the equivalent of seventeen university degrees, in the sciences and arts," Flint said. "She is aware that the intellect is not all—but its development must come first, or the individual makes errors, wastes time in unprofitable pursuits."

"At her age, I rather enjoyed my errors," said McCoy. "But, no damage done, obviously, Rayna. You're the farthest thing from a bookworm I've ever seen."

"Flint is my teacher. You are the first other humans I have ever seen."

Kirk stared at her, not sure he liked what he had heard. But it was none of his business.

"The misfortune of men everywhere," McCoy was saying, "is our privilege."

Flint said, "If you would accompany my robot to the

laboratory, Doctor, you can be assured that the processing of the ryetalyn is well in hand."

McCoy picked up the ryetalyn cubes and looked uncertainly at M-4. The robot turned silently in midair and glided out, the surgeon in tow.

"Your pleasure, gentlemen?" Flint said. "Chess? Billiards? Conversation?"

Kirk was still staring at Rayna. "Why not all three?" he said absently.

Kirk was no pool shark, and found Rayna far better at it than he was. He lined up a shot, intent. Flint and Spock watched.

Flint said, "I have surrounded Rayna with the beautiful and the good of human culture—its artistic riches and scientific wisdom."

Kirk muffed the shot.

"I have protected her from its venality—its savagery," Flint went on. "You see the result, Captain."

Rayna had lined up a three-cushion shot, which paid off brilliantly. Kirk straightened, feeling resigned.

"Did you teach her *that?*" he asked.

"We play often."

"May I show you, Captain?" Rayna said. She stepped close to him, correcting his grip on the cue.

"You said savagery, Mr. Flint," Kirk said. "How long is it since you visited Earth?"

"You would tell me that it is no longer cruel. But it is, Captain. Look at your Starship—bristling with weapons . . ."

Kirk and Rayna were bending, close together, their arms intertwined on the cue as she set him up for the shot. He found that not much of his mind was on Flint.

". . . its mission to colonize, exploit, destroy if necessary, to advance Federation causes."

Kirk made the shot. This time it was a pretty good one.

"Our missions are peaceful," he said, "our weapons defensive. If we were such barbarians, we would not have *asked* for the ryetalyn. Your greeting, not ours, lacked a certain benevolence."

"The result of pressures that are not your concern."

Spock had wandered over to the piano and sat down, studying the manuscript on the music rack.

"Such pressures are everywhere," Kirk said, "in every man, urging him to what you call savagery. The private hells—the inner needs and mysteries—the beast of instinct. As humans, we'll always be that way." He turned to Rayna, who seemed surprised that anyone would dare to argue with Flint. "To be human is to be complex. You can't escape a little ugliness, inside yourself and from without. It's part of the game."

Spock began casually to pick out the melody of the music manuscript. Flint looked toward him, seemingly struck by a sudden notion, "Why not play the waltz, Mr. Spock?" He turned to Kirk. "To be human is also to seek pleasure. To laugh—to dance; Rayna is a most accomplished dancer."

Sight-reading, Spock began to play. Kirk looked at Rayna. "May I have the pleasure?"

She went into his arms. The first few steps were clumsy, for Kirk was somewhat out of practice, but she was easy to lead. She was wearing a half smile of seeming curiosity. Flint watched them both, outwardly paternal, but also speculatively.

Spock was doing very well, considering that the manuscript looked hastily written; but there was something in his intentness that suggested more than mere concentration on the problems of reading the notation.

As Kirk and Rayna whirled past Flint, she gave Flint a bright, pleased smile, more animated than any expression she had shown before. Flint returned the smile with apparent affection—but there was still that intent speculation underneath.

Then McCoy entered, looking very grim indeed. Spock stopped playing, and the dancing couple broke apart.

"Something wrong?" Kirk asked.

"Nothing to dance about. The ryetalyn is no good! We can't use it. It contains irillium—nearly one part per thousand."

"Irillium would make the antitoxin inert?" Spock said.

"Right. Useless."

"Most unfortunate that it was not detected," Flint said. "I shall go with M-4 to gather more ryetalyn and screen it myself. You are welcome to join me, Doctor." He went out, evidently to summon the robot.

"Time factor, McCoy?" Kirk said. "The epidemic?"

"A little over two hours and a half. I guess we can get in under the wire. I've never seen anything like the robot's speed, Jim. It would take us twice as long to process the stuff."

"Would we have made the error?" Kirk asked grimly.

"*I* made the error, just as much as the robot. I didn't suspect the contaminant until scanning the completed antitoxin showed it up. What if all the ryetalyn on this planet contains irillium?"

"Go with Flint. Keep an eye on procedures."

"Like a hawk," McCoy said, turning away. "That lab's an extraordinary place, Jim. You and Spock should have a look."

He went up the ramp after Flint. Spock got up from the piano bench, picking up the manuscript.

"Something else which is extraordinary," he said. "This waltz I played is by Johannes Brahms. But it is in manuscript, Captain—written in Brahms' own hand, which I recognize. It is an unknown waltz—absolutely the work of Brahms—but unknown."

"Later, Mr. Spock," Kirk said, preoccupied. "I think I will take a look at that laboratory. All our lives depend upon it. If we could get the irillium out of the existing antitoxin . . . Where did Rayna go?"

"I did not see her leave, Captain. I was intent upon . . ."

"All right. Stay here. Let me know when McCoy and Flint return."

Spock nodded and sat down again at the piano. As Kirk went up the ramp, the strains of the waltz began to sound again behind him.

He found the laboratory without difficulty, and it was indeed a wonder, an orderly mass of devices only a few of which looked even vaguely familiar. What use did Flint ordinarily have for such an installation? It implied research work of a high order and constantly pursued. Was there no limit to the man's intellectual resources?

Then Kirk realized that he was not alone. Rayna was standing on the other side of the lab, before another door. Her hands were clasped before her and her eyes were raised in an attitude of meditation, or of questioning for which she could not find the words. But she seemed also to be trembling slightly.

Kirk went to her, and she turned her head. Yes, she was shivering.

"You left us," Kirk said. "The room became lonely."

"Lonely? I do not know the word."

"It is a condition of wanting someone else. It is like a thirst—like a flower dying in a desert." Kirk halted, surprised at his own outburst of imagery. His eyes looked past her to the door. "What's in there?"

"I do not know. Flint has told me I must never enter. He denies me nothing else."

"Then—why are you here?"

"I—do not know. I come to this place when I am troubled—when I would search myself."

"Are you troubled now?"

"Yes."

"By what?" She looked intently and searchingly into his eyes, but did not answer. "Are you happy here, with Flint?"

"He is the greatest, kindest, wisest man in the Galaxy."

"Then why are you afraid? You *are* afraid; I can see it." He put his arms around her protectively. The trembling did not stop. "Rayna, this place is cold. Think of something far away. A perfect, safe, idyllic world—your presence would make it so. A world that children dream of . . ."

"Did I dream? My childhood—I remember this year—last year . . ."

What had Flint done to this innocent? He felt his expression hardening. She looked bewildered. "Don't be afraid," he said gently. He kissed her. It was meant to be only a brotherly kiss, but when he drew back, he found that he was profoundly shaken. He bent his head to kiss her more thoroughly.

As he did, her gaze flashed over his shoulder, and her eyes widened with horror. "No!" she cried. "No, no!"

Kirk whirled, belatedly aware of the whirring of the robot. The machine was floating toward him, lights flashing ominously. He put himself between the robot and the girl. It advanced inexorably, and he backed a step, trying to lead it away from Rayna.

"Stop!" Rayna cried. "*Stop!*"

M-4 did not stop. Kirk, backtracking, ducked beind a

large machine and pulled out his phaser; when the robot appeared, he fired point-blank. As he had more than half expected, the weapon failed to work.

"Stop! Command! *Command!*"

Steadily, the robot backed Kirk into a corner. He braced himself to rush it—futile, without doubt, but there was no other choice.

Then there was the hissing snap of a phaser, and the robot vanished.

Spock appeared from around the corner of the massive machine where Kirk had tried to ambush M-4, stowing his phaser.

"Whew," Kirk said. "Thank you, Mr. Spock."

"Fortunately the robot was too intent on you to deactivate my phaser," Spock said. "Dr. McCoy and Mr. Flint have returned with the ryetalyn."

Was Rayna all right? Kirk went to her. She seemed unharmed. Suddenly she lifted a hand to touch his lips. Then she turned away, wide-eyed, deep in troubled thoughts.

They were back in the central room—Spock, Rayna, and a very angry Kirk. Flint was quite calm. Behind his back, Spock had his tricorder out and aimed at him.

"M-4 was programmed to defend this household, and its members," Flint said calmly. "No doubt I should have altered its instructions, to allow for unauthorized but predictable actions on your part. It thought you were attacking Rayna. A misinterpretation."

Kirk was far from sure he bought that explanation. He took a step toward Flint.

"If it was around now, it might interpret quite correctly . . ."

Whirrrr.

The machine was back—or an exact duplicate of it, floating watchfully near Flint.

"Too useful a device to be without, really," Flint said. "I created another. Go to the laboratory, M-5."

Spock stowed his tricorder over his shoulder. "Matter from energy," he said. "An almost instantaneous manufacture, no doubt, in which your robot was duplicated from an existing matrix."

Flint nodded, but he did not take his eyes from Kirk.

"Be thankful that you did not attack me, Captain. I might have accepted battle—and I have twice your physical strength."

"In your own words, that might be an interesting test of power."

"How childish he is, Rayna. Would you call him brave—or a fool?"

"I am glad he did not die," Rayna said in a low voice.

"Of course. Death, when unnecessary, is tragic. Captain, Dr. McCoy is in the laboratory with the new ryetalyn. He is satisfied as to its purity. I suggest that you wait here, patiently—safely. You have seen that my defense systems operate automatically—and not always in accordance with my wishes."

Kirk felt a certain lack of conviction about this last clause.

Flint put his hand on Rayna's arm. "Come, Rayna."

After a last, long look at Kirk, she allowed herself to be led up the ramp. Scowling, Kirk took a stubborn step after them, but Spock held him back.

"I don't like the way he orders her around," Kirk said.

"Since we are dependent upon Mr. Flint for the ryetalyn, I might respectfully suggest, Captain, that you pay less attention to the young lady, should you encounter her again. Our host's interests do not appear to be confined to art and science."

"He loves her?" Kirk said.

"Strongly indicated."

"Jealousy! That could explain the attack. But still—he seemed to *want* us to be together; the billiards game—*he* suggested that we dance . . ."

"It would seem to defy the logic of the human male, as I understand it."

After an uneasy moment, Kirk brought out his communicator. "Kirk to *Enterprise*. Mr. Scott, report on the Rigellian fever."

"Nearly everybody aboard has got it, sir. We're working a skeleton crew, and waiting for the antitoxin."

"A little while longer, Scotty. Report on computer search."

"No record of Mr. Flint. He simply seems to have no past. The planet was purchased thirty years ago by a Mr. Nova, a wealthy financier and recluse."

"Run a check on Rayna Kapec. Status: legal ward, after death of parents."

"Aye, Captain."

As Kirk slowly put the communicator away, Spock said, "There is still a greater mystery. I was able to secure a tricorder scan of Mr. Flint, while you and he were involved in belligerence. He is human. But there are biophysical peculiarities. Certain body-function readings are disproportionate. For one thing, extreme age is indicated—on the order of six thousand years."

"Six thousand! He doesn't look it, not by a couple of decimal places. Can you confirm that, Mr. Spock?"

"I shall program the readings into Dr. McCoy's medical computer when we return to the ship."

"Time factor?"

"We must commence antitoxin injections within two hours and eighteen minutes, or the epidemic will prove fatal to us all."

Kirk frowned. "Why is the processing taking so long this time?"

"The delay would seem to be possibly deliberate."

"Yes," Kirk said grimly. "As if he were keeping us here for some reason."

"Most strange. While Mr. Flint seems to wish us to linger, he is apprehensive. It is logical to assume that he knows our every move—that he has us monitored."

The communicator beeped. "Kirk here."

"Scott, sir. There's no record of a Rayna Kapec in the Federation legal banks."

"No award of custody?"

"No background on her at all, in any computer bank. Like Flint."

"Thanks, Scotty. Kirk out. Like Flint. People without a past. By what authority is she here, then? What hold does he have over her?"

"I would suggest," Spock said, "that our immediate concern is the ryetalyn."

"Let's find McCoy."

As they headed for the door, Rayna entered. She seemed to be agitated. "Captain!" she called.

"Go ahead, Spock, I'll meet you in the laboratory."

When they were alone, Rayna said, "I have come to say goodbye."

"I don't want to say goodbye."

"I am glad that you will live."

Kirk studied her. She seemed innocent, uncertain, yet underneath there was a kind of urgency. She stood motionless, as if in the grip of forces she did not understand.

He went to her. "I know now *why* I have lived." He put his arms around her and kissed her. This second kiss was much longer than the first, and her response suddenly lost its innocence.

"Come with us," Kirk said hoarsely.

"My place . . ."

"Is where you want to be. Where do you want to be?"

"With you."

"Always."

"Here," she said.

"No, come with me. I promise you happiness."

"I have known security here."

"Childhood ends. You love *me*, not Flint."

For a long moment she was absolutely silent, hardly even seemed to breathe. Then she broke free of his arms and ran off. Kirk stared after her, and then started off to the laboratory, his heart still pounding.

The moment Kirk entered, McCoy said, "Flint lied to us. The ryetalyn isn't here."

"But I am picking up readings on the tricorder, Captain," Spock said. "The ryetalin is apparently behind that door."

The door toward which the tricorder was aimed was the same one Rayna had said Flint had forbidden her to enter.

"Why is Flint playing tricks on us?" Kirk demanded, suddenly furious at the constant multiplication of mysteries. "Apparently we're supposed to go in and get it—if we can! Let's not disappoint the chessmaster. Phasers on full!"

But as the weapons came out, the door began to rumble open of its own accord. A constant, low hum of power was audible from inside it.

Kirk lead the way. The ryetalyn cubes were conspicuously visible on a table. Kirk went toward them in triumph, but his attention was caught by a draped body encased on a slab. The slab carried a sign which read: "RAYNA 16."

The body was the supine form of a woman. The face was not quite human; it resembled dead white clay, beautifully sculptured and somehow unfinished. Nevertheless, it was clearly Rayna's.

Hung on the other side of the case was a clipboard with notes attached. Most of the scribbles seemed to be mathematical.

As if in a dream, Kirk moved on to a similar case. The figure in it was less finished than the first. Its face seemed to show marks of sculpture; the features were more crudely defined. Still, it too was Rayna's—Rayna 17.

"Physically human," McCoy said in a low voice, "yet not human. These are earlier versions. Jim—she's an android!"

"Created here, by my hand," Flint's voice said from the doorway. "Here, the centuries of loneliness were to end."

"Centuries?" Kirk said.

"Your collection of Leonardo da Vinci masterpieces, Mr. Flint," Spock said. "Many appear to have been recently painted—on contemporary canvas, with contemporary materials. And on your piano, a waltz by Johannes Brahms, an unknown work, in manuscript, written with modern ink—yet absolutely authentic, as are the paintings . . ."

"I am Brahms," Flint said.

"And da Vinci."

"Yes."

"How many other names shall we call you?" Spock asked.

"Solomon, Alexander, Lazarus, Methuselah, Merlin, Abramson—a hundred other names you do not know."

"You were born . . . ?"

"In that region of Earth later called Mesopotamia—in the year 3034 B.C., as the millennia are now reckoned. I was Akharin—a soldier, a bully and a fool. I fell in battle, pierced to the heart—and did not die."

"A mutation," McCoy said, fascinated. "Instant tissue regeneration—and apparently a perfect, unchanging balance between anabolism and katabolism. You learned you were immortal . . ."

"And to conceal it: to settle and live some portion of a life; to pretend to age—and then move on, before my nature was suspected. One night I would vanish, or fake my demise."

"Your wealth, your intellect, the product of centuries of study and acquisition," Spock said. "You knew the greatest minds of history . . ."

"Galileo," Flint said. "Moses. Socrates. Jesus. And I have married a hundred times. Selected, loved, cherished—caressed a smoothness, inhaled a brief fragrance—then age, death, the taste of dust. Do you understand?"

"You wanted a perfect woman," Spock said. "An ultimate woman, as brilliant, as immortal, as yourself. Your mate for all time."

"Designed by my heart," Flint said. "I could not love her more."

"Spock," Kirk whispered, "you knew."

"Readings were not decisive. However, Mr. Flint's choice of a planet rich in ryetalyn—I had hoped I was wrong."

"Why didn't you tell me?" Kirk asked harshly.

"What would you have said?"

"That you were wrong," Kirk said, "*wrong*. Yes, I see."

"You met perfection," Flint said. "Helplessly, you loved it. But you cannot love an android, Captain. *I* love her; she is my handiwork—my property—she is what I desire."

"And you put the ryetalyn in here to teach me this," Kirk said. "Does she know?"

"She will never know."

Kirk said tiredly, "Let's go, Mr. Spock."

"You will stay," Flint said.

"Why?"

"We have also learned what *he* is, Captain."

"Yes," said Flint. "If you leave, the curious would follow—the foolish, the meddlers, the officials, the seekers. My privacy was my own; its invasion be on your head."

"We can remain silent," Spock suggested.

"The disaster of intervention, Mr. Spock. I've known it—I will not risk it again." Flint's hand went to a small control box on his belt.

Kirk whipped out his communicator. Flint smiled, almost sadly. "They cannot answer, Captain. See."

A column of swirling light began to form slowly in a clear area of the life chamber. As it brightened, the form of the *Enterprise* was revealed, floating a few feet above the floor, tiny familiar lights blinking.

"No!" Kirk cried.

"The test of power," Flint said. "You had no chance."

"My crew . . ."

"It is time for you to join them."

Kirk felt sick. "You'd—wipe out—four hundred lives? Why?"

"I have seen a hundred million fall. I know Death better than any man; I have tossed enemies into his grasp. But I know mercy. Your crew is not dead, but suspended."

"Worse than dead," Kirk said savagely. "Restore them! Restore my ship!"

"In time. A thousand—two thousand years. You will see the future, Captain Kirk." Flint looked at the *Enterprise*. "A fine instrument. Perhaps I may learn something from it."

"You have been such men?" Kirk said. "Known and created such beauty? Watched your race evolve from cruelty and barbarism, throughout your enormous life! Yet now, you would do *this* to us?"

"The flowers of my past. I hold the nettles of the present. I am Flint—with my needs."

"What needs?"

"Tonight I have seen—something wondrous. Something I have waited for—labored for. Nothing must endanger it. At last, Rayna's emotions have stirred to life. Now they will turn to me, in this solitude which I preserve."

"*No,*" said Rayna's voice. They all spun around.

"Rayna!" Flint said in astonishment. "How much have you heard?"

"You must not do this to them!"

"I must." Flint's hand moved implacably back to the belt device.

"Rayna," Spock said. "*What will you feel for him—when we are gone?*"

She did not reply, but the expression of betrayal, tragedy, and bitter hatred which she turned on Flint was answer enough.

All emotions are engaged, Mr. Flint," Spock said. "Harm us, and she hates you."

"Give me my ship," Kirk said coldly. "Your secret is safe with us."

Flint looked at Kirk levelly. Then there was the slightest suggestion of a shrug; here was a man who had lost battles before. He touched the belt control again.

The column of light with the toy *Enterprise* in it faded and vanished.

"That's why you delayed processing the ryetalyn," Kirk said, in a low, bitter voice. "You realized what was happening. You kept us together—me, Rayna—because I could make her emotions come alive. Now you're going to just take over!"

"I shall take what is mine—when she comes to me," Flint said. "We are mated, Captain. Alike immortal. You must forget your feelings in this matter, which is quite impossible for you."

"Impossible from the beginning," Kirk said in growing fury. "Yet you used me. I can't love her—but I do love her! And *she loves me!*"

Flint sprang. He was quick, but Kirk evaded him. The two combatants began circling like animals. As Kirk passed Spock, the First Officer seized his arm.

"Your primitive impulses cannot alter the situation."

"*You* wouldn't understand! We're fighting over a woman!"

"You are *not*," Spock said, "for *she* is not."

Kirk stepped back, turning his palms out toward his adversary. "Pointless, Mr. Flint."

"I will not be the cause of all this," Rayna said, in a voice both fiery and shaken. "I will not! I choose! I choose! Where I want to go—what I want to do! *I choose!*"

"I choose for you," Flint said.

"No longer!"

"Rayna . . ."

"*No*. Don't order me! *No* one can order me!"

Kirk looked at her in awe, and it seemed as though Flint was feeling the same sensation. He extended a hand toward her, and she turned from it. He dropped the hand slowly, staring at her.

"She's human," Kirk said. "Down to the last blood cell, she's human. Down to the last thought, hope, aspiration, emotion. You and I have created human life—and the human spirit is free. You have no power of ownership. She can do as she wishes."

"No man beats me," Flint said coldly.

"I don't want to beat you," Kirk said wearily. "There's no test of power here. Rayna belongs to herself now. She claims her human right of choice—to do as she will, think as she will, *be* as she will."

Finally Flint gave a tired nod. "I have fought for that also. What does she choose?"

"Come with me," Kirk said to her.

"Stay," said Flint.

There were tears in her eyes. "I was not human," she whispered. "Now, I love—I love . . ."

She moved slowly forward toward the two waiting men. She seemed exhausted. She stumbled once, and then, suddenly, fell.

McCoy was at her side in an instant, feeling for her pulse. Flint also knelt. Slowly, McCoy shook his head.

It hit Kirk like a blow in the stomach. "What—happened?" he asked.

"She loved you, Captain," Spock said gently, "and also Flint, as a mentor, even a father. There was not time enough to adjust to the awful powers and contradictions of her newfound emotions. She could not bear to hurt either of you. The joy of love made her human; its agony destroyed her." In his voice there was a note of calm accusation. "The hand of God was duplicated. A life was created. But then—you demanded ideal response—for which God still waits."

Flint bowed his head, a broken man. "You can't die, we will live forever—together." He sobbed. "Rayna—*child* . . ."

Kirk's hand moved, almost blindly, to his shoulder.

Kirk sat at his desk in his own cabin, in half light, exhausted, brooding. The door opened and Spock came in.

"Spock," Kirk said, and looked away.

"The epidemic is reduced and no longer a threat. The *Enterprise* is on course 513 mark seven, as you ordered."

"The very young and lonely man—the very old and lonely man—we put on a pretty poor show, didn't we?" He bowed his head. "If only I could forget . . ."

His head went down on his arms. He was asleep.

McCoy entered in full cry. "Jim, those tricorder readings of Mr. Flint are finally correlated. Methuselah is dying . . ."

Then he noticed Kirk's position, and added in a low voice, "Thank Heaven—sleeping at last."

"Your report, Doctor?" Spock said.

"Flint. In leaving Earth, with its complex of fields in which he was formed and with which he was in perfect balance, he sacrificed immortality. He'll live the remainder of a normal life-span—and die."

"That day, I shall mourn. Does he know?"

"I told him myself. He intends to devote his last years, and his gigantic abilities, to improving the human condition. Who knows what he might come up with?"

"Indeed," Spock said.

"That's all, I guess. I'll tell Jim when he wakes up, or you can." He looked at Kirk with deep sympathy. "Considering his opponent's longevity—truly an eternal triangle. You wouldn't understand, would you, Spock? I'm sorrier for you than I am for him. You'll never know the things love can drive a man to—the ecstasies, the miseries, the broken rules, the desperate chances—the glorious failures, and the glorious victories—because the word love isn't written in your book."

Spock was silent.

"I wish he could forget her." Still silence. "Good night, Spock."

"Good night, Doctor."

Spock regarded Kirk for another silent moment, and then moved deliberately to lock the door behind McCoy. Then he returned to Kirk. His hands floated to Kirk's dropped head, fingertips touching. He said, very gently, "*Forget . . .*"

THE WAY TO EDEN

(Arthur Heinemann and Michael Richards)

Under Federation orders to observe extreme delicacy, the *Enterprise* had beamed aboard the six people who had stolen the cruiser *Aurora*. The son of the Catullan Ambassador was one of them, and treaty negotiations between the Federation and the Ambassador were at a crucial phase. Clearly, none of the six had known much about operating a cruiser; in the attempt to escape, they had managed to destroy the cruiser, and had only been rescued by Scott's pinpoint skill with the Transporter.

"Scotty, are they aboard?" Kirk asked his control chair intercom.

"Aye, Captain, they are. And a nice lot, too."

"Escort them to the briefing room for interview."

There were other voices in the background, rising in an increasing hubbub. Suddenly a woman's voice became clearly audible above the others. "Why should we?"

At that, Chekov's head jerked up sharply, his expression one of recognition struggling with incredulity. Then a man's voice said, "Tell Herbert it's no go."

All the voices chimed in with a ragged chant: "No go no go no go no go . . ."

"What's going on?" Kirk asked.

"They refuse, sir," Scott called over the chant.

"Why?"

"I don't know. They're just sitting on the floor, the lot of them. You can hear them yourself. Shall I send for Security?"

"No, I'll come down. Sulu, take the con."

He and Spock could hear the chanting continuing long before he reached the Transporter Room. The six were, indeed, "a nice lot." One wore a simple robe, the others were nearly naked or in primitive costumes, with flowers worn as ornaments and painted on their bodies. There were three girls and three men, all but the one in the robe in their early twenties. They were squatting on the floor with a clutter of musical instruments around them.

"We are not in the mood, Herbert," one of the girls said; it was the same voice he had heard before. The others resumed the "No go" chant.

"Which one of you is Tongo Rad?" Kirk shouted.

The chant died down raggedly, and the newcomers looked curiously from Kirk to one of their number, a handsome humanoid who despite his costume had that intangible air which often goes with wealth and privilege. He got up and lunged forward, not answering, not quite insolent.

"You can thank your father's influence for the fact that you're not under arrest," Kirk snapped. "In addition to piracy, you're open to charges of violating flight regulations, entering hostile space and endangering the lives of others as well as your own."

"Hostile space?" Rad said.

"You were in Romulan territory when we yanked you out."

"Oh," said Rad. "I'm bleeding."

"On top of which you've caused an interstellar incident that could destroy everything that has been negotiated between your planet and the Federation."

"You got a hard lip, Herbert."

"If you have an explanation, I'm prepared to hear it."

Rad looked down at the older man in the robe, but there was no response. Rad sat down with the others and folded his arms.

Kirk turned to Spock. "Take them to sickbay for medical check. There may be radiation injury from the *Aurora* explosion."

The "No go" chant started up again immediately. Kirk started to shout, but Spock intervened.

"With your permission, Captain." He put his hands together, index finger to index finger, thumb to thumb, forming an egg shape. "One."

The group seemed to be surprised. The man in the robe rose. "We are one."

"One is the beginning," Spock said.

One of the boys, a rather puckish youth, said, "You One, Herbert?"

"I am not Herbert."

"He's not Herbert. We reach."

Kirk was wholly bewildered. Evidently all this meant something, however, and had almost miraculously achieved calm and accord.

"Sir," Spock said to the older man, "if you will state your purpose and objectives, perhaps we can arrive at mutual understanding."

"If you understand One, you know our purpose."

"I should prefer that you state it."

The older man smiled faintly. "We turn our backs on confusion and seek the beginning."

"Your destination?"

"The planet Eden."

"Ridiculous," Kirk said. "That planet's a myth."

Still smiling, the older man said, "And we protest against being harassed, pursued, attacked, seized, and Transported here against our wishes and against human law."

"Right, brother," said the puckish youth.

"We do not recognize Federation regulations nor the existence of hostilities. We recognize no authority but that within ourselves."

"Whether you recognize authority or not, I am it on this ship," Kirk said, restraining himself with difficulty. "I am under orders to take you back to Starbase peaceably. From there you will be ferried back to your various planets. Because of my orders you are not prisoners, but my guests. I expect you to behave as such."

"Oh, Herbert," said the puckish youth, "you are *stiff*."

"Mr. Spock, since you seem to understand these people, you will deal with them."

"We respectfully request that you take us to Eden," the robed man said. Despite the politeness of the words, and the softness of his voice, his insolence was obvious.

Kirk ignored him. "When they're finished in sickbay, see that they are escorted to the proper quarters and given whatever care they need."

"Yes, Captain."

"We respectfully request that you take us to Eden."

"I have orders to the contrary. And this is not a passenger ship."

"Herbert," said the girl who had first spoken. The others picked it up and another ragged chant followed Kirk as he went out: "Herbert Herbert Herbert Herbert . . ."

He was in a simmering rage by the time he returned to the bridge. Taking his seat, he said, "Lieutenant Uhura. Alert Starbase we have aboard the six who took the space cruiser *Aurora*. And that the cruiser itself was regrettably destroyed."

"Aye, sir."

"Personal note to the Catullan Ambassador. His son is safe."

"Captain, sir," Chekov said hesitantly. "I believe I know one of them. At least I think I recognized her voice. Her name is Irina Galliulin. We were in Starfleet Academy together."

"One of those went to the *Academy*?" Kirk said incredulously.

"Yes, sir. She dropped out. She—" Chekov stopped. Under his accent and his stiffness, it was apparent that he still felt a painful emotion about this girl.

Kirk looked away as Spock entered, and then back to Chekov. "Do you wish to see her? Permission granted to leave your post."

"Thank you, sir." He got up fast and left; another crewman took his post.

Kirk turned to Spock. "Are they in sickbay?"

"Yes, Captain."

"Do they seriously believe that Eden exists?"

"Many myths are founded on some truth, Captain. And they are not unintelligent. Dr. Sevrin . . ."

"Their leader? The man in the robe?"

Spock nodded. "Dr. Sevrin was a brilliant research engineer in acoustics, communications and electronics on Tiburon. When he started the movement, he was dismissed from his post. Young Rad inherits his father's extraordinary abilities in the field of space studies."

"But they reject that—everything this technology provides—and look for the primitive."

"There are many who are uncomfortable with what we have created," Spock said. "It is almost a biological rebellion. A profound revulsion against the planned communities, the programming, the sterilized, artfully balanced atmospheres. They hunger for an Eden, where Spring comes."

"We all do, sometimes," Kirk said thoughtfully. "The cave is deep in our ancestral memories."

"Yes, sir."

"But we don't steal cruisers and act like irresponsible children. What makes you so sympathetic toward them?"

"It is not so much sympathy as curiosity, Captain. A wish to understand. And they regard themselves as aliens in their worlds. It is a feeling I am familiar with."

"Hmm. What does Herbert mean?"

"It is somewhat uncomplimentary, sir. Herbert was a minor official notorious for his rigid and limited pattern of thought."

"I get the point," Kirk said drily. "I shall endeavor to be less limited in my thinking. But they make it difficult."

There were only five of the six in the examining room when Chekov came in. Four were sprawled about listening to the puckish youth, who was tuning something that looked like a zither. Apparently satisfied, he hit a progression of chords and began to sing softly.*

> Looking for the new land—
> Losing my way—
> Looking for the good land—
> Going astray—
> Don't cry.
> Don't cry.
> Oh I can't have honey and I can't have cream

*I much regret that I cannot reproduce the music which went with this script; it was of very high quality. The script I have does not name the composer.—J.B.

But the dream that's in me, it isn't a dream.
It'll live, not die.
It'll live, not die.
I'll stand in the middle of it all one day,
I'll look at it shining all around me and say
I'm here!
I'm here!
In the new land,
In the good land,
I'm here!

"Great, Adam," one of the others said. There was a murmur of applause.

Chekov cleared his throat. "Excuse me. Is Irina Galliulin with you?"

"Getting her physical," Adam said. He hit a chord and sang:

I'll crack my knuckles and jump for joy—
Got a clean bill of health from Dr. McCoy.

"You know Irina?" someone else said. Chekov nodded.

"Say, tell me," said Tongo Rad. "Why do you people wear all those clothes? How do you breathe?"

Nurse Chapel came out of the sickbay with two medics. She looked over the group and pointed to Sevrin. "You're next."

Sevrin sprawled, oblivious. Chapel nodded to the two medics, who stepped forward and, picking up the limp form, dragged it into sickbay. A moment later, Irina came out.

"Irina," Chekov said.

She did not seem to be surprised. She smiled, her strange, habitual smile, which rarely left her—but there was watchfulness behind it.

"Pavel Andreievich," she said calmly. "I had thought we might encounter each other."

"You knew I was on the *Enterprise*?"

"I had heard."

"Irina—why—" He stopped, all eyes upon him. "Come."

He led her out into the corridor, which was empty. He stared at her for a moment, taking in the bizarre, brief costume, the long hair, the not-quite-untidiness. When he spoke, it was almost with rage.

"How could you do this to yourself? You were a scientist. You were a—a decent human being. And now look at you!"

"Look at yourself, Pavel," she said calmly.

"Why did you do it?"

"Why did you?"

"I am proud of what I am. I believe in what I do. Can you say that?"

"Yes." Momentarily her voice was sharp; then the smile returned. Chekov took her arm and they walked toward the lounge. "We should not tear at each other so. We should meet again in joy. Today, when I first knew it was your ship that followed us, I thought of you, I wondered what I would find in you. And I remembered so much. In spite of that uniform, I still see the Pavel I used to know. Are you happy in what you do?"

"Yes."

"Then I accept what you do."

"You even talk like them."

Yeomen passed them, turning to look at the odd couple. Chekov led Irina into the lounge. "Why did you go away?" he asked.

"It was you who went."

"I came back to look for you. I looked. I looked. Where did you go?"

"I stayed in the city. With friends."

"You never felt as I did. Never."

"I did."

"You don't have it in you to feel so much. Even when we were close you weren't with me. You were off thinking of something else." She shook her head, the smile still there. "Then why did you stay away?"

"Because you disapproved of me. Just as you do now. Oh, Pavel, you have always been like this. So correct. And inside, the struggle not to be. Give in to yourself. You will be happier. You'll see."

"Go to your friends," Chekov said grayly.

After a moment she left, still with that maddening smile. There seemed to be another hubbub starting in the corridor. Chekov went after her, quickly.

The noise was coming from outside sickbay, where there was something very like a melee going on. The group from the *Aurora* was trying to get in, over the opposition of Nurse Chapel and two security guards. The group was shouting noisily, angrily, demanding entrance, demanding to see Sevrin.

Kirk came out of the elevator and forced his way through the crowd, not without a what-the-[illegible] glance toward Chekov.

"Herbert Herbert Herbert Herbert Herbert . . ."

The sickbay doors shut automatically behind Kirk and Nurse Chapel, mercifully deadening the sound. "I thought all those animals were in their cages," she said.

Sevrin was sitting on a bed, defiant, the two medics standing ready to grab him. McCoy was finishing what had evidently been a strenuous examination.

"What's going on, Bones?"

"Trouble. Your friend here didn't want a checkup. Turns out there was a reason."

"I refuse to accept your findings," Sevrin said.

"You don't have the choice."

"They are the product of prejudice, not science."

"I don't know what this man was planning to do on a primitive planet," McCoy continued. "Assuming it existed. But I can tell you what would happen if he'd settled there. Within a month there wouldn't be enough of those primitives left to bury their dead."

"Fantasy," Sevrin said. "Fantasy."

"I wish it were. There's a nasty little bug evolved in the last few years, Jim. Our aseptic, sterilized civilizations produced it. *Synthococcus novae*. It's deadly. We can immunize against it but we haven't licked all its problems yet."

"Does he have it?" Kirk asked. "What about the others?"

"The others are clear. And he doesn't have it. He's a carrier. Remember your ancient history? Typhoid Mary? He's immune to it, as she was. But he carries the disease, spreads it to others."

"Is the crew in danger?"

"Probably not. They all had full spectrum immunizations before boarding. My guess is that his friends had their shots too. But a regular program of booster shots is necessary. I'll have to check on everyone aboard. There may have been some skips. Until that's done, this fellow should be kept in total isolation."

"This is outrageous," Sevrin said. "There is nothing wrong with me. You're not isolating me, you're imprisoning me. You invent the crime, find me guilty, sentence me . . ."

"Would you like to run the tests yourself, Doctor?" There was no answer. "You knew you were a carrier before you started out, didn't you?"

"No!"

"Then why did you fight the examination?"

"It was an infringement on my rights as a human being . . ."

"Oh, stop ranting."

"Put him in isolation," Kirk said.

"Be ready for his friends' objections. They're a vocal lot."

"I'm ready."

There was still a crowd in the corridor; four of the *Aurora* group (one girl was missing) were sitting or sprawling on the deck; among them stood Sulu, Chekov and several crewmen. The protesters were chanting, but this time each of them had a different slogan.

"Edon now!"

"Free Ton Sevrin!"

"James T. Kirk is a brachycephalic jerk!"

"McCoy is a doctor of veterinary medicine!"

Sulu was talking to one of the girls, between slogans. He seemed confused but fascinated. Thus far no one had noticed Kirk's arrival.

"You don't belong with them," the girl was telling Sulu. "You know what we want. You want it yourself. Come, join us."

"How do you know what I want, Mavig?"

"You're young. Think young, brother." Lifting a hand to him, she gave him an egg.

"Mr. Sulu," Kirk said sharply. Sulu started, stiffened with embarrassment, and hastily gave the egg back to Mavig. "Explain, Mr. Sulu."

"No explanation, sir."

Kirk turned to the group, which had gotten even noisier upon seeing him. "Dr. Sevrin will be released as soon as we determine it is medically safe."

"Herbert Herbert Herbert Herbert . . ."

Ignoring them, Kirk strode toward the elevator with

Sulu, stepping over the bodies. Chekov followed. As he approached Irina, she lay back provocatively.

"Don't stay with Herbert. Join us. You'll be happier. Come, Pavel."

"Link up, Pavel," Adam said.

"Join us."

"Link up, Pavel. Link up, Pavel."

Adam struck a chord on his instrument and began to sing:

> Stiff man putting my mind in jail—
> Judge bangs the gavel, and says
> No bail—
> So I'll lick his hand and wag my tail . . .

Blessedly the elevator doors opened at this point, and Kirk, Sulu and Chekov made their escape.

The bridge was a haven of routine activity, with Spock in charge. Chekov and Sulu went to their posts. But before Kirk could settle, the intercom cut in with its signal.

"Engineering to bridge," Scott's voice said.

"Kirk here."

"Captain, I just had to give one of those barefooted what-do-you-call-ems the boot out of here. She came in bold as brass, tried to incite my crew to disaffect."

"All right, Scotty." He shut the intercom off and turned to Spock, his irritation finally breaking out. "Mr. Spock, I don't seem to communicate with these people. Do you think you can persuade them to behave?"

"I shall endeavor, sir."

"If it weren't for that Ambassador's son, they'd be in the brig."

"Yes, sir." Spock went out.

He found Sevrin sitting cross-legged in the isolation ward, in a yoga-like position, a cold, hostile figure. There was one security guard in the corridor outside. Spock stood on the other side of the isolation shield.

"Doctor, can you not keep your people from interfering with the running of the ship?"

"I have no influence over what they do."

"They respect you. They will listen to your reasoning. For their sake, Doctor, you must stop them."

The baleful eyes lifted to Spock's face, answer enough in themselves.

"Dr. Sevrin, I can assist you and your group. I can use the resources of the *Enterprise* to establish whether or not Eden exists, and to plot its exact location. I can present a case to Federation that would allow your group to colonize that planet." There was no answer. "Neither you nor they are at present charged with any crime worse than theft, plus a few lesser matters. The charges may be waived. But incitement to mutiny would tip the balance. And Federation would never allow the colonization of a planet by criminals. If they persist, they will be so charged, and forever barred from Eden."

"As I have been barred," Sevrin said softly. The voice was low, but the gleaming eyes were those of a fanatic.

Spock hesitated a moment. "Then you knew you were a carrier?"

"Of course I knew. You have researched my life. You have read the orders restricting me to travel only in areas of advanced technology, because of what my body carries."

"I fail to understand why you should disobey them."

"Because this is poison to me!" Sevrin looked around, as if seeing all the technology of the ship, representing all the technology of space. "This stuff you breathe, this stuff you live on. The shields of artificial atmosphere we have layered about every planet. The programs in those computers that run your ship and your lives for you. Those bred what my body carries! This is what your sciences have done for me! You have infected me!"

He shook his fist at the ceiling; his "you" was obviously not Spock but the whole Galaxy. He began to pace.

"Only the primitives can cleanse me. I cannot purge myself until I am among them. Only their way of living is right. I must go to them."

"Your very presence will destroy the people you seek out! Surely you know that."

"I shall go to them and be one of them. Together we will make a world such as this Galaxy has never seen. A world, a life. A life!" His passion spent, Sevrin sat down, and after a moment lifted his head to look at Spock, a faint smile on his lips. "And now you are about to assure me that your technologies will find a cure for me. And I will be free to go."

"Yes, Doctor."

"And for that reason I must persuade my friends to behave, so they too will be allowed."

"Yes."

"Send them in," Sevrin said, smiling still. "I'll talk to them."

It was an uneasy victory, whose outcome was uncertain. Spock went back to the bridge.

"They've been a lot quieter," Kirk reported. "How did you accomplish it?"

"It had nothing to do with me. Could I speak to you a moment, sir?"

Kirk rose and both went to Spock's console. "What is it?"

"Dr. Sevrin is insane. I did not consult Dr. McCoy. But I have no doubt of it."

"I'll have Bones check him again," Kirk said, stunned. "You had great respect for him. I'm sorry, Mr. Spock. But it explains some of what they've done."

"His collapse does not affect my sympathy with the moevment, sir. There is no insanity in what they seek—I made a promise which I should like to keep. With your permission, I must locate Eden. I shall work in my quarters. May I have the assistance of Mr. Chekov in the auxiliary control room?"

"Mr. Chekov, assist Mr. Spock."

The auxiliary control room was deserted except for Chekov, who was at the plotting console, bent over the computer, studying.

Spock's voice came over the intercom. "Ready for your plottings, Mr. Chekov."

Chekov fed a tape into the computer. The door opened, and Irina entered, hesitantly. "Am I allowed in?" she asked.

He concentrated stiffly on his work. "Yes."

"I have been looking for you, Pavel. What room is this?"

"Auxiliary control."

"What's it for?"

"Should the main control room break down or suffer damage, we can navigate the ship from here."

"Oh."

"What do you want?"

"To apologize. I should not have teased you. It was cruel."

"It doesn't matter," Chekov said.

"But it does. It is against everything I believe in."

"Let us not discuss your beliefs."

"And I do not like having you angry with me," she said softly. "Or disapproving."

"Then why do you do such things?"

She began to wander about the room, examining the panels in seeming childlike curiosity. Chekov continued working, but his eyes followed her when she was not looking in his direction. Then she came back to him. "What are you working on?"

"I am assisting Mr. Spock in locating your Eden."

"Now you are teasing me," she said in sudden sharpness.

"I am not. These tapes contain star charts, and we project the orbits of the various known planetary systems here, determining by a mathematical process whether or not they are affected by other bodies not yet charted."

"Do you know all these things?"

"What I do not know I find out from the computer banks. If I knew nothing at all, I could navigate this ship simply by studying what is stored in there. They contain the sum of all human knowledge. They solve our problems of navigation, of control, of life support . . ."

She bent over the computer, close to him. "They tell you what do do. And you do what they tell you."

"No. We use our own judgment also."

She came still closer. "I could never obey a computer."

"You could never listen to anyone. You always had to be different."

"Not different. What I wanted to be. There is nothing wrong in doing what you want."

She faced him, smiling still. Abruptly Chekov arose, took her in his arms, and kissed her hungrily.

"I am not receiving, Mr. Chekov," said the intercom. "Spock to Mr. Chekov. Repeat. I am not receiving."

Chekov broke free and opened his intercom. "I am sorry, Mr. Spock. I was momentarily delayed."

With permission, the *Aurora* group had stored its gear and bedded down in the Recreation Room. Adam and Mavig were relaxing when Rad entered.

"His name is Sulu," Rad said. "Specialist in weapons and navigation. His hobby is botany."

"Can?" said Adam.

"Can. I reach botany. It's my favorite of studies. What's yours?"

"Vulcan. Spock is practically One now."

Irina came in; the others were instantly alert.

"Everything can be handled from auxiliary control. The computers contain all the information we need. We can do it."

"It starts to chime," Adam said.

"When will it?" Rad wanted to know.

"Soonest. Like Sevrin said, now, we should go out, swing as many over as we can."

"You suggest any special ways to swing them?"

"Just be friendly. You know how to be friendly, then they'll be friendly and we'll all be one. All right? Scatter. Remember, it's a party we're inviting them to and we're providing the entertainment."

"I like parties," Rad said.

"I like the entertainment we've planned. All hit numbers."

Adam and Rad grinned at each other. Then everyone went off, in different directions. Adam headed directly for Spock's quarters.

Spock said "Come in" absently. He was at his computer, studying the images, making notes. Adam approached him diffidently.

"Am I crossing you?" he asked. Spock shook his head. "I was wondering if—" He stopped, noting the lute hanging on the wall behind Spock. "Hey, brother. You play?"

Spock nodded.

"Is it Vulcan? Can I try it?"

Spock took the lute down and gave it to Adam, who tried several chords. "Oh, that's now. That's real now. I reach that, brother, I really do. Give."

He passed the lute back to Spock, who amusedly played a few runs.

"Hey. How about a session, you and us. It would *sound.* That's what I came for. I wanted to ask, you know, great white captain up there he don't reach us, but would he shake on a session? I mean, we want to cooperate like you asked, so I'm asking."

"If I understand you correctly," Spock said, "I believe the answer might be yes."

"I'll spread the word."

The Recreation Hall was jammed. Lights had been dimmed, with the effect of spotlighting the group. They were singing: for those crew members who could not be present, intercoms carried the music throughout the ship. The words went like this:

> I'm talking about you.
> I'm talking about me.
> Long time back when the Galaxy was new,
> Man found out what he had to do.
> Found he had to eat and found he had to drink,
> And a long time later he found he had to think.
>
> *(spoken)*
> I'm standing here wondering.
>
> *(sung)*
> If a man tells another man, 'Out of my way'
> He piles up trouble for himself all day.
> But all kinds of trouble come to an end
> When a man tells another man, 'Be my friend.'
>
> *(spoken)*
> What's going to be?
>
> *(sung)*
> There's a mile wide emptiness between you and me,
> Can't reach across it, hardly even see—
> Someone ought to take a step one way or other.
> Let's say goodbye—or let's say brother.
> Hey out there
> Hey out there
> I see you
> I see you
> Let's get together and have some fun.
> Don't know how to do it but it's got to be done.

There was enthusiastic applause. The three girls took up the song. The boys faded back, clapping rhythmically. The clapping soon spread throughout the audience.

On the bridge, Uhura, Sulu and Scott were at their

posts, listening. When Kirk came in, Uhura turned the intercom off.

"Thank you."

"At least we know where they are and what they're doing," Scott said. "I don't know why a young head has to be an undisciplined one. Troublemakers."

"I made a bit of trouble at that age, Scotty. I think you may have."

The intercom buzzed. "Spock to bridge."

"Go ahead."

"Captain, something strange is taking place. Two of the boys slipped out of the group somewhere during the last five minutes, and now the girls are beginning to go. And it is not Haydn's Farewell Symphony they are staging, either."

"Come to the bridge."

"Something strange here too," Sulu said. "I have no response on controls. We're going off course."

Scott crossed to Sulu's console and checked it. "It's shorted—no, it's channeled over somewhere—yes, to auxiliary control."

As Spock entered, Kirk began calling. "Bridge to auxiliary control. Bridge to auxiliary control."

"Captain," Spock said, "in my opinion someone else is running the ship."

"That's right, Captain," said Sevrin's voice from the intercom. "Someone else is running the ship. I am. All functions, Captain. Life support as well. I suggest that you do not attempt to regain control. I do not intend to return the helm to you until and unless we reach Eden. If I am in any way prevented from reaching that destination, I shall destroy the ship and all aboard."

Scott and Sulu had been frantically checking circuits. Now Scott said, "He can do it, Captain. He has got everything channeled over."

"Start a traceback on all circuits. See if you can bypass."

"Do that," Sevrin's voice said, "and I shall retaliate. I shall not warn you again."

"We are leaving the neutral zone now, Captain," Sulu said. "Bearing into Romulan space."

"Do you read any patrols, Mr. Spock?"

"No, sir."

"They'll be on us soon enough. Dr. Sevrin! You are violating Romulan space and endangering the peace of the Galaxy. They will see this as a military intrusion and attack. Bring her about. Now. If you bring her about and return to Starbase, nothing will be said about this."

"Like you said, brother Sevrin," said Adam's voice.

"If you do not, you will never reach Eden. You and this ship will be destroyed. We would be no match for a Romulan flotilla."

"He's got jelly in the belly," said Adam. "Real scared."

"Adam, Rad—you are being led by a man who is insane. You are being used by him. Spock, tell them."

"Adam," Spock said. "There is a file in the computer banks on Dr. Sevrin. You will find in it a report attesting to the fact that he is a carrier of a bacillus strain known as *Synthococcus novae*."

"Ain't that just awful?"

"You will also find a report from the same hospital giving a full psychiatric profile of him, projecting these actions of his."

"Yeah, brother."

"You know I reach you," Spock said. "I believe in what you seek. But there is a tragic difference between what you want and what he wants."

"You're making me cry," Adam said. Then he began to sing:

> Heading out to Eden—
> Yeah, brother!
> Heading out to Eden—
> Yeah, brother!
> No more trouble in my body or my mind—
> I'll live like a king on whatever I find—
> Eat all the fruit and throw away the rind—
> Yeah, brother!"

Kirk shut off the intercom; it was impossible even to try to determine a course of action through that noise. He got up and looked at Spock, who nodded.

"We are within sensor range of Eden and continuing to approach," he said.

"Whatever they're going to do, they'll do it now," Kirk said. "We have no choice left. Mr. Spock, Mr. Scott, come with me. And let's make it fast."

He led them down the corridors to auxiliary control.

"Phasers out and on full. We'll cut through the door. If Sevrin stops Life Function, we should be able to get through and start it again before any serious consequences follow—I hope. We'll take shortcuts in turn, so as not to risk killing somebody and damaging equipment when we hole through. I'll go first, then Spock, then Scott."

His phaser spat, followed by Spock's. Then another sound started, like the whine of an oscillator, going higher and higher. Spock, with his sensitive hearing, reacted first. He dropped his phaser and clapped his hands to his ears.

"Mr. Spock!" As Kirk went to him the sound stopped. "It has stopped. It's all right, Mr. Spock."

"It—hasn't stopped—Captain. It is beyond—no! Captain—they are using . . ."

Kirk's head suddenly swam. If there was an end to Spock's sentence, he never heard it.

An unknown time later, Kirk came to, finding the corridor just as before, Spock and Scott stirring to consciousness. No, not just as before; the door to auxiliary control was open, and there was no one in there.

The three of them got to their feet and staggered in. Spock pointed. "There it is. An ultrasonic generator, feeding into the ventilation system . . ."

The First Officer suddenly leaped forward and smashed the device with an iron first.

"Why did you do that?" Kirk said. "The parts could have . . ."

"It was set to go off again in a few seconds, Captain—and this time on a killing frequency. It must have been Sevrin's work; I doubt that the youngsters would have let him do it had they known the device could be made lethal. Clearly he didn't intend us to get back to make any reports."

Kirk grabbed the intercom and began calling. "Kirk to bridge. Come in, do you read me? Engineering. Hangar deck. Transporter Room. Do you read me? Kirk to bridge."

"Captain?" Scott's voice said.

"Sulu here, Captain. What happened to us? I heard a whistle and then . . ."

"Never mind, Sulu," Kirk said. "Do we have control of the ship?"

"It's still all in auxiliary, sir," said Chekov's voice. "Some of the gear is jammed."

"Can we break orbit if we have to?"

"I think so, sir."

"Hangar deck to Captain."

"Kirk here."

"Sir, one of the shuttlecrafts has been taken. We were all knocked out . . ."

"Stand by. Mr. Spock, do you read any Romulans?"

"Negative, Captain. I am picking up the shuttlecraft, however."

"Where?"

"It has landed. Sir, except for those aboard the shuttlecraft, I read no sign of life at all. Neither animal nor humanoid. And there are only five life forms aboard the craft."

"Auxiliary control to McCoy. Bones, are you all right?"

"Yes, Jim."

"Stand by the Transporter Room. Full medical gear."

"Bridge to Captain Kirk," said Uhura's voice. "Do you wish hailing frequency, sir?"

"No. They tried to destroy us. Let them think they succeeded. I want coordinates zeroed in so that when we beam down we are not visible to them. Mr. Scott, the con is yours. If a Romulan patrol appears, hold in orbit; Lieutenant Uhura is to try to make them understand. I don't want to provoke combat. Mr. Chekov, join us in the Transporter Room. Mr. Spock, you too."

The garden was brilliant with sunshine, dazzling with flower color, opulent with heavy-laden fruit trees, one of them a giant. But it was utterly silent. The landing party looked about in awe.

"The legends were true, sir," Spock said in a low voice. "A fantastically beautiful planet."

"Eden," said Chekov.

Kirk said, "It almost—was this what they believed they'd find?" Spock nodded. "I can understand now. But why have they remained in their ship? Well, spread out and approach with caution."

The other three moved away. Kirk remained where he

was, flipping open his communicator. "Dr. Sevrin, this is Captain Kirk. You are under arrest. You will debark from your ship."

The shuttlecraft remained silent, its doors shut. Then there came a whimpering little sound, in Irina's voice. "No . . ."

"You will come out at once."

"No! No!" This time it was a scream of pure terror. Kirk went after McCoy.

"Bones, you heard that? What do you make of it?"

"She sounds terrified."

"Of what?"

McCoy took out his tricorder. "I don't know, Jim. I don't read anything abnormal. Wait a minute . . ."

There was a yell of pain from Chekov. He was standing by a flowering plant, his right fist clenched to his chest, his face contorted. They got to him fast.

"What is it, Chekov?"

"The flower, sir. I touched it. It's like fire."

McCoy forced him to unclench the fist. Fingers and palm were stained and seared. The surgeon aimed the tricorder at it, then at the flower, the plant proper, the grasses.

"The sap in it is pure acid," McCoy said. "All the plant life. The grass, too." He took out his medical kit and smeared ointment over Chekov's hand.

"Their feet!" Kirk said. "They were barefoot! Don't touch a thing. Bones, will our clothing protect us?"

"For a short time."

"Captain," Spock called. "Come over here, please."

He was standing under the largest fruit tree. Kirk joined him and looked down. Adam lay dead on the ground, twisted, a half-eaten piece of fruit from the tree still clutched in his hand.

"Bones," said Kirk.

McCoy took readings. "Poison. The fruit is deadly."

Spock bent and picked up the body, his enormous strength holding it easily. He looked at Kirk. "His name was Adam."

Understanding now, Kirk walked to the shuttlecraft openly, Spock beside him. Kirk pushed a button, and the doors opened. He called in gently, "You will be cared for."

The girls and Rad came limping out, murmuring in pain.

"It hurts," Irina said.

"I know," Spock said. "It hurts us all."

Chekov went at once to Irina and held her comfortingly as McCoy began to treat her. Kirk went on inside the craft.

Dr. Sevrin sat on the deck in the yoga position, immobile, heedless of his blistered, naked feet. His injuries were shockingly worse than those of the others.

"Bones, in here, please! Dr. Sevrin—Dr. Sevrin. Look at him, Bones. How can he stand it?"

"He should be beamed aboard. He needs more attention than I can give him here."

"No!" Sevrin said suddenly. "No. We are not leaving."

"We'll take care of you aboard the ship," Kirk said.

"We are not leaving Eden. None of us."

"Be sensible, Sevrin."

"We're not leaving!" As Kirk bent to help him, Sevrin thrust him savagely aside, lunged for the door and ran, despite the agony it must have cost him. He plunged straight toward the huge fruit tree. There was no chance of stopping him; by the time Kirk and McCoy were out of the craft, he had reached the tree, seized a fruit and bitten into it.

"No! I have found my Eden!"

Then he moaned, doubled, and fell.

The group by the shuttlecraft were for a moment paralyzed by shock. Then Chekov turned to Irina. "He too is dead, Irina."

She looked at him in a daze. "And the dream is dead. He sacrificed so much for it. When we landed, and he saw Eden finally, he cried, all of us felt the same. It was so beautiful. And we ran out into it—and . . ."

"Spock to *Enterprise*. Mr. Scott, stand by to beam the injured aboard. Medical team to the Transporter Room."

Everything was normal again on the bridge. Uhura said, "I have Starbase now, Captain."

"Alert them that we have the four and will be beaming them down. And mark the incident closed."

"Yes, sir."

"Bridge to Transporter Room. Scotty, are they there?"

"Three of them, sir."

"Stand by. Mr. Chekov, do you wish to attend?"

Chekov stood hesitantly. "Captain, sir, I wish first to apologize for my conduct during this time. I—did not maintain myself under proper discipline. I endangered the ship and its personnel by my conduct. I respectfully submit myself for disciplinary action."

"Mr. Chekov," Kirk said with a faint smile. "You did what you had to. As all of us did. Even your friends. You may go."

"Thank you, sir."

He started for the elevator, but as he did so, the doors opened and Irina stepped out. For a moment they looked at each other in silence.

"I was coming to say goodbye," Chekov said.

"And I was coming to say goodbye to you."

They kissed, gently, sadly. Irina said, "Be incorrect, occasionally."

"And you be correct."

"Occasionally."

She turned back to the elevator, but was intercepted by Spock. "Miss Galliulin, it is my sincere wish that you do not give up your search for Eden," he said. "I do not doubt but that you will find it—or make it yourselves."

She bowed her head, entered the elevator and was gone. Chekov and Spock went back to their posts. Chekov still seemed to be caught in the moment; then he became aware of the silence about him, the awareness of the others. He looked around.

Kirk was smiling faintly; he turned to Spock, whose face was expressionless, but who was nodding.

Kirk said, "We reach, Mr. Chekov."